Natural Selection

A Collection of Short Stories

By

Nina Munteanu

Pixl Press

Natural Selection: a collection of short stories

Copyright © 2013 Nina Munteanu

All rights reserved. No part of this book may be reproduced or transmitted in any form or by any means, electronic or mechanical, including photocopying, or recording, or by any information storage and retrieval system, without permission in writing from the publisher, except by a reviewer or academic who may quote brief passages in a review or critical study.

Cover Illustration: Anne Moody
Cover Design and Typology: Costi Gurgu
Interior Design: Nina Munteanu

Published in Canada by Pixl Press
an imprint of Starfire World Syndicate, Louisville, KY, USA

Library and Archives Canada Cataloguing in Publication

Munteanu, Nina [Short stories. Selections]   Natural selection : a collection of short stories / Nina Munteanu.

Issued in print and electronic format.
ISBN 978-0-9811012-8-6 (pbk.)
ISBN 978-0-9811012-9-3 (mobi)

I. Title. II. Title: Short stories. Selections

PS8626.U68A6 2013   C813'.6   C2013-902188-4

C2013-902189-2

For Lari

Acknowledgements

I am grateful to Paul Agosto, who published my first short story ("Arc of Time" in *The Armchair Aestthete*). It sparked a creative fire for the short story form that has burned inside me to this day. Those who have stoked those flames over the years include David Lee Summers, Steve Stanton, Karl Johanson, Brett Alexander Savory and Paul G. Tremblay, Arkadiusz Nakoniecznik, Blazej Dzikowski, Mircea Pricăjan, Gary Markette, John C. Snider, and Lari Davidson. I admire their faith in maintaining the short story form through magazines, anthologies and webzines.

Although some have come and gone, the dedication that has persisted draws from the recognition that in some ways the short story is the highest form of storytelling, with a power to transport, disturb and enlighten.

I also thank Heidi Lampietti, publisher and editor of Redjack Books, for her impeccable editorial comments on these short stories prior to making their way into this collection.

Praise for Nina Munteanu's previous works:

"Nina Munteanu is ... a master of metaphor ... a creator of fantastic worlds and cultures. She combines her biological background with the infinite possibilities of the cosmos and turns an adventure story into a wonderland of alien rabbit holes."
> — **Craig H. Bowlsby**, author of *Horth in Killing Reach* and creator of *Commander's Log*

"*Angel of Chaos* is a gripping blend of big scientific ideas, cutthroat politics and complex yet sympathetic characters that will engage readers from its thrilling opening to its surprising and satisfying conclusion."
> — **Hayden Trenholm**, Aurora-winning author of *The Steele Chronicles*

Darwin's Paradox is "a thill ride that makes us think and tugs the heart."
> — **Robert J. Sawyer**, Hugo-Award authot of *Wake*

Angel's Promises is "a stunning example of good storytelling with an excellent setting and cast of characters."
> — **Tangent Online**

Collision with Paradise is" a very intelligent story, with fantastic world-building."
> — **Romantic Times**

"Munteanu asserts her mastery of the sensual SF romantic thriller. [*Collision with Paradise* is] an unforgettable read that's immensely alluring, surprising, and heart-throbbing."
> — **Yet Another Book Review**

Table of Contents

Author's Introduction

Evolution is the language of destiny. What is destiny, after all, but self-actualization and synchronicity? If evolution is the language of destiny, then choice and selection are the words of evolution and "fractal ecology" is its plot.

How do we define today a concept that Darwin originated 200 years ago in a time without bio-engineering, nano-technology, chaos theory, quantum mechanics and the Internet? We live in an exciting era of complicated change, where science based on the limitation of traditional biology is being challenged and stretched by pioneers into areas some scientists might call heretical. Endosymbiosis, synchronicity, autopoiesis & self-organization, morphic resonance, Gaia Hypothesis and planetary intelligence. Some of these might more aptly be described through the language of meta-physics. But should they be so confined? It comes down to language and how we communicate.

Is it possible for an individual to evolve in one's own lifetime? To become more than oneself? And then pass on one's personal experience irrevocably to others—laterally and vertically?

On the vertical argument, the French naturalist Jean-Baptiste Lamark developed a theory of biological evolution in the early 19th century considered so ridiculous that it spawned a name: Lamarkism. His notion—that acquired traits could be passed along to offspring—was ridiculed for over two hundred years. Until he was proven right. Evolutionary biologists at Tel Aviv University in Israel showed that all sorts of cellular machinery—an intelligence of sorts—played a vital role in how

6

DNA sequences were inherited. When researchers inserted foreign genes into the DNA of lab animals and plants, something strange happened. The genes worked at first; then they were "silenced". Generation after generation. The host cells had tagged the foreign genes with an "off switch" that made the gene inoperable. And although the new gene was passed onto offspring, so was the off switch. It was Larmarkism in action: the parent's experience had influenced its offspring's inheritance. Evolutionists gave it a new name. They called it *soft inheritance*.

As for passing on one's experience and acquisitions to others laterally, education in all its facets surely provides a mechanism. This may run the gamut from wise mentors, spiritual leaders, storytellers, courageous heroes to our kindergarten teacher. Who's to say that these too are not irrevocable? This relies, after all, on how we learn, and how we "remember".

Evolution is choice. It is a choice made on many levels, from the intuitive mind to the intelligent cell. The controversial British botanist Rupert Sheldrake proposed that the physical forms we take on are not necessarily contained inside our genes, which he suggested may be more analogous to transistors tuned in to the proper frequencies for translating invisible information into visible form. According to Sheldrake's morphic resonance, any form always looks alike because it 'remembers' its form through repetition and that any new form having similar characteristics will use the pattern of already existing forms as a guide for its appearance. This notion is conveyed through other phenomena, which truly lie in the realm of metaphysics and lateral evolution; concepts like bilocation, psychic telegraphing, telekinesis and manifestation. Critics condemn these as crazy notions. Or is it just limited vision again? Our future cannot be foretold in our present language; *that* has yet to be written. Shakespeare knew this...

> *There are more things in heaven and earth,*
> *Horatio, than are dreamt of in your philosophy—*
> Shakespeare

The nine stories contained herein touch on many of these concepts, spanning a 20-year writing period starting in the 1980s from "Arc of Time", first published by *The Armchair Aesthete* in 2002, to "Julia's Gift", written in 2007, a year that marks a significant nexus in my personal evolution. That's when I met someone who changed my life and defined my life path, my evolution, and ultimately, I suspect, my destiny.

Each story reflects a perspective on what it means to be human and evolve in a world that is rapidly changing technologically and environmentally. How we relate to our rapidly changing fractal environments—from our cells to our ecosystems, our planet and ultimately our universe—will determine our path and our destiny and those we touch in some way. My friend Heidi Lampietti, publisher of Redjack Books, expressed it eloquently, *"For me, one of the most important themes that came through in the collection is the incredible difficulty, complexity, and importance of making conscious choices—and how these choices, large and small, impact our survival, either as individual humans, as a community, a species, or a world."*

Each story touches on a focal point, a nexus in someone's personal evolution, where a decision—or an indecision—will define one's entire later path in life. Several stories (e.g., "Butterfly in Peking", "Frames" and "Julia's Gift" all set in the same universe as my "Darwin's Paradox" duology) explore this through war: a paradoxical struggle between those who follow the technological path and those who embrace nature's intelligence. War is itself a paradox. It is both tragedy and opportunity. The very action of being at war seems to galvanize us and polarize us. War heightens contrast, increases pitch, and resonates through us in ways we have no inkling. It brings out the very worst but also the very best in us; for, as some of us sink into despair and self-serving debauchery, others heroically rise in altruistic service and humble sacrifice to help others. War defines us, perhaps like no other phenomenon.

Several stories are quirky adapted excerpts from my two books, "Darwin's Paradox" (2007 by *Dragon Moon Press*) and its prequel "Angel of Chaos" (2010 by *Dragon Moon Press*). You will find some of the same characters there, though names have been changed to protect the innocent. You will also find the sprawling semi-underground AI-run city of Icaria (a post-industrial plague Toronto) and a character itself. Several of the characters portray "gifted" and troubled misfits—outcasts, anti-heroes, artists not in sync with the rest of the population. Yet how that person's choices—and how s/he is treated by their community—would influence an entire species or world ("Mark of a Genius", "Neither Here Nor There", "Angel's Promises", and "Natural Selection").

Lastly, I explore how humanity evolves, communicates and relates through forces larger than itself, either produced through its own making via technology (in "Virtually Yours") or through timeless universal intervention (in "Arc of Time"). The last story (in fact the first written) provides a very different interpretation of an old biblical myth about new beginnings and our cyclical destiny of "creative destruction".

I hope you enjoy reading them all. I enjoyed writing them.

"The Arc of Time" was first published in the Summer/Fall 2002 issue of *The Armchair Aesthete*. It was reprinted in *Imagikon* (2003) then scheduled for the premiere issue of *Ultra!* A charity issue dedicated to cystic fibrosis (Aardwolf Publications), Fall/Winter, 2004. Sadly, Lari Davidson, the editor and visionary behind the project passed away suddenly and the issue never came to fruition.

"Virtually Yours" first appeared in Issue 15 (December 2002) of *Hadrosaur Tales*. It was reprinted in *Neo-Opsis Science Fiction Magazine* (Issue 3, Spring 2004) then translated into Polish and reprinted in the January 2006 issue of *Nowa Fantastika* (Poland). It was translated into Hebrew and reprinted in *Bli-Panika* (Israel) in 2006. "Virtually Yours" was selected for the 2006 "The Best of Neo-Opsis Science Fiction Magazine" anthology (*Bundoran Press*) and was nominated for the Canadian

Aurora Prix and the Speculative Literature Foundation Fountain Award.

"Angel's Promises" was published in Issue #30 (March, 2003) of *Dreams & Visions* then selected for the anthology "Skysongs II: Spiritual SF" (2005). It was nominated for the SLF Fountain Award.

"A Butterfly in Peking" was first published in Issue #17 (2003) of *Chiaroscuro*. It was translated into Polish and reprinted in the Summer 2005 issue of *Nowa Fantastika* (Poland) then translated and reprinted in *The Dramaturges of Yann* (Greece) in 2006.

"Mark of a Genius" first appeared in *Scifidimensions* (August 2004 issue) and "Neither Here Nor There" first appeared in *Another Realm* (September 2005). "Frames", "Julia's Gift" and "Natural Selection" make their first appearance here.

Virtually Yours

Vincent yanked the V-set off his head and found himself back in his apartment, lying alone and spent on his king-size bed. The cozy cabin with the fireplace had vanished. Katherine was gone.

He stared at the V-set. His vehicle to paradise. To Katherine.

Her scent of lilac lingered in his mind as he summoned her beautiful face, smiling just for him. No, he reminded himself. *Not for me. For Jake, my carrier.* It was Jake she smiled at. Jake she had just made love to. Jake, who smelled her desire, felt the tender stroke of her slender legs. Vincent was just along for the ride.

His eyes swept down his deformed and gnarled body. Angry boils and scars encrusted his livid hairless skin. He remembered colliding two days ago with her in a Samson Corporation hallway and her hand had unintentionally brushed his thigh. She'd jerked back, blushing with the shame of not knowing how to avoid staring at him in revulsion. Then she'd rushed off before he had a chance to speak. Probably to wash her hand.

I'm just another anonymous Corporation Overseer, he thought. A nameless ugly gnome. She doesn't know that I'm Vincent, her Overseer, with whom she shares beautiful thoughts of life and poetry over the V-screen.

Two weeks ago she'd boldly offered a few friendly

11

comments at the end of her progress memo. He'd responded with his own and found himself looking forward to her messages more than anything else during the workday. When he opened them, he clicked straight to her post-script, leaving her formal report for later. He recalled the message she'd sent him last week that had started everything:

"Do you like poetry, Overseer? It is one of my passions. I've read a lot of Milton lately. Granted his writing is over 400 years old; yet he evokes in my soul a yearning for Eden. Do you think Eden can exist on Earth? Perhaps it is our destiny to long for it."

Up to then she'd used her worker code-name as salutation: "Cheers, V-screen USER 134872". This time she'd signed, "Virtually yours, Katherine."

It was as he reread her signature over and over, that he'd come up with his ingenious scheme to track her down among the hundred roaming workers in the Samson Corporation research lab: he'd assign a carrier to work with her. It had started out innocently enough. He'd only wanted to know what she looked like. It was SenTech's fault.

His SenTech holo program and the V-set's link to a sensor embedded in Jake's forehead gave Vincent the next best thing to having Katherine. Thanks to Jake, who didn't even know he was providing Vincent this service, SenTech permitted Vincent to see, hear, feel and taste Katherine using Jake's senses. Jake had no idea of Vincent's access to the implant or that Overseers typically used them to spy on their carriers. Jake only knew that the implant provided him with enhanced cognitive abilities. Being connected directly to the central computer database was a great advantage to him in his work as Vincent's data manager.

Hoping to make the meeting pleasant for her, as well as for himself, Vincent had selected Jake as his carrier based on what he'd ascertained of Katherine's physical tastes in men. But once he saw her blush with desire at Jake's perfect physique, smelled her hunger and felt Jake's heart throb, he knew that he'd wanted more all along. This would be a good ride, he'd thought, and immediately prepared his AIs for full surveillance.

Jake moved fast. Following their initial inflamed encounter at Samson Corp, Jake enticed her to his secluded cabin, where he seduced her. Vincent was unprepared for the sweetness of it and how it inflamed his own forgotten desires. Through Jake, Vincent felt like a consummate lover, drawing her out patiently, using gentle, tender strokes at first then matching her escalating rhythm. She was shy though not coy and wonderfully responsive. When the lovemaking had ended, Vincent felt strange, as though he'd betrayed himself. Moved by the experience, he'd wrenched off his V-set and wrote her an E-note as her anonymous Overseer. He'd heavily quoted Milton.

"She'd never look at me the way she looks at Jake," Vincent said, glancing down at his misshapen body. Mildred, his model 20 AI droid, glided to the bed and touched his shoulder. It said in a tinny voice, "She does not know you are her Overseer, Vincent? Perhaps you should tell her, she might like you—"

"No, Mildred," he snapped. He imagined compassion in Mildred's round green eyes and let his voice soften, "She might like communicating with me as her anonymous Overseer, but I'm afraid this is the only way she'll ever look at me *that* way." He placed the V-set on the nightstand. "She could never love *me*." Vincent let out a long breath and stroked the V-set. "But I'm content with what I have." A wry smile crossed his lips as he wrestled with a pleasure edged in guilt. His creative use of SenTech's surveillance capabilities definitely stretched its intended use. "Does that make me some sort of pimp?" He eyed the folds in the sheets then stroked the sheet. Resting his gaze on the leopard-skin of his hand, he murmured, "So be it. At least I'm a harmless one."

"The library inquires as to whether you wish to save this SenTech scenario as Katherine One for later use?" Mildred inquired.

"Yes, yes," he said impatiently. He brought the sheet to his face, wanting to savor her scent, knowing he would smell nothing, and clenched the fabric into a ball. With a cursory glance down at his gnarled body, he jerked to his feet. "Save it."

Φ

"He's so damn ugly. Like some monster from a bad movie," Fanny whispered to Katherine as they looked for free workstations. Fanny stared through the transparent panel to a hunched figure in the office perched above them. He was one of twenty Overseers in the Research Department of Samson Corporation, but Katherine knew which one Fanny meant. There was only one ugly Overseer.

She stole a glance up to where he paced like a feral cat, eyes flashing at them. She felt her face heat. Embarrassed for him, she quickly looked away. Of course he hadn't heard Fanny. But surely he knew what they all said about him. Could read it in their churlish glances and smirks. The glabrous skin of his face and head looked like melted wax. Its smooth surface was blemished with islands of angry bubbles and crevasses that resembled burning lava. She couldn't help thinking of the rumor that he'd actually caused the fire, which had nearly taken his life and killed several people. They'd been experimenting with a new product at the lab. The explosion took his three colleagues, including his fiancée.

"You wonder why he doesn't get some major surgery done," Fanny continued as they claimed two unoccupied workstations. "In this day and age, when nano-reconstruction's so attainable, it's as if he *wants* to look that way, to scare us all."

Punishing himself, Katherine thought, and felt her eyes sting. If Fanny could only look beyond his ugly shell into those eyes of gentle sadness and vulnerability. She remembered when they'd bumped into one another three weeks ago in the hallway and her hand had accidentally touched his thigh. He smelled of smoke and metal. Their eyes met and she blushed like a teenager. He had the eyes of a poet. She'd turned away without a word and fled. He'd probably thought her rude.

"Fanny, he's probably a G-type," Katherine said, glaring into space. She yanked at her chair and let herself drop into it. "G-types can't handle the side effects of nano-construction." Her fingers slid furiously along the alpha console, activating her virtual support and accessing the network with her code. Instantly, her station housed itself with a set of files, a virtual bookshelf filled with books, and a vase with flowers.

"Okay," Fanny said, settling into the chair next to her. She activated her virtual support: stacks of files with documents and papers and a poster of a naked man. "You don't have to get snippy about it. You'd think you liked him or something." She gazed into the distance. "I'm glad we don't know who our Overseers are—or they us. I'd die if he turned out to be mine. Imagine if he was *your* Overseer, Katherine! How awful! What irony: beauty and the beast. It's like he knows it too, knows how absurd that would be—he never looks at you."

Katherine felt her face crimson. Or was it that he detested physical beauty? Found her reprehensible?

Fanny leaned into her and cocked her head. "He might as well be an AI20, alone up there in his ivory tower, anonymously giving orders to some of us peons. Ugly as sin and cold as metal."

Katherine recoiled. "Fanny!" She focused on her computer screen, surprised at the yearning that stirred inside her. He wasn't a machine. More like a wounded animal. No one knew the name much less the identity of his or her Overseer. But when she'd defied protocol two weeks ago and signed with her name, he'd followed suit with his: Vincent. She knew Vincent was the beast up in the tower. Felt it in her heart. Vincent's "voice" and the beast's eyes spoke the same truth. But where the ignoble beast howled baleful regrets to the moon, this beast quoted poetry to her.

No, not to *her*, she corrected herself. She was just another rude employee who bumped into him once. He didn't know she was V-screen USER 134872—now Katherine—who sent him progress memos, and lately shared her personal thoughts with him. She clicked on her saved messages and found the one she was looking for, Vincent's response three weeks ago to her brazen remark about poetry and Milton. She'd delivered it out of her frustration with corporate conformity and a foolish longing for something "more"; she hadn't expected such a stirring response.

She'd reread it several times and every time her heart flipped when he used her name:

"I admire your passion for poetry, Katherine. Does it not strip prose to the very essence of what drives our soul? If you believe in destiny, then each of us is already a story waiting to be written; mine would be a tragedy. My burning desire for knowledge destroyed the thing I most loved. I do not expect to find Eden in my lifetime here on this Earth, or elsewhere, for that matter.

"You have made me curious to read Milton. His poetry remains relevant to this day. Perhaps you are right about our longing for Eden: *'These lull'd by Nightingale embracing slept, and on their naked limbs the flow'ry roof show'r'd roses, which the morn repair'd'.*"

Following her lead, he'd signed "Virtually yours, Vincent."

Three weeks later they were still sharing personal philosophies and always found an opportunity to quote Milton.

"Now, that's more like it!" Fanny's strident voice cut into her silent rapture. Katherine jumped in her seat, swept the screen clear and looked up, face burning in anticipation of finding Fanny looking over her shoulder. But Fanny was gazing at a man striding toward them. Katherine sighed and felt a surge of pleasure. Jake. She'd met him just over two weeks ago, when Vincent had assigned them a joint task.

"Now there's a specimen." Fanny said. "What a perfect body and face. Bet he's a great lay."

Katherine blushed. She appraised Jake's showman's eyes, firm jaw that easily supported the loose smile he always wore, and a seamless brow partially hidden beneath thick curls of chestnut hair. Yes, he was a knock out. And exciting.

"You're a lucky girl." Fanny sighed.

"Yeah," Katherine said, sensing her own hesitation. "Lucky." Although they'd been physically intimate many times already, she still didn't know Jake. His charm and humor masked a reserve of quiet depth—or nothing? Could he sustain a loving relationship with her or was Jake just lustfully infatuated with her?

"He's a carrier, isn't he?"

Katherine nodded. "Carries a piece of the V-net inside him."

"That's why he's so swift and enlightened."

Katherine nodded. She didn't consider Jake exactly enlightened. Swift, perhaps. He'd managed to get her in a prone position the first day they met and every day after that.

"You're so lucky, Katherine. You've got it all."

Katherine swallowed. She'd been considering breaking it off. Jake seemed more interested in using his mouth for kissing than for talking. After two weeks of wonderful sex, she began to long for the serenity that came with sharing an ordinary life with another person. She and Jake didn't seem to have much in common. They'd never conversed like she and Vincent had on the V-screen. Jake was a bored realist. And he took no interest in poetry.

She resolved to break it off, before he dumped her for another lustful jaunt.

"Hi, girls." Jake tussled Fanny's mop then glided to

Katherine like a panther. Gathering her long hair back with both hands, he bent to kiss her on the neck. Her decision blurred at his seductive touch. Jake seized her hands and coaxed her up from her seat. "Come." He grinned like a boy hiding a lizard in his pocket. "I have something to tell you." He led her away from the workstations toward the lounge.

"What is it, Jake?" Her eyes darted around her and she looked annoyed at him. "People are watching."

"I can't tell you here. Tonight. Meet me at Samson Square, Level Two, at twenty-three hundred. That's when my evening shift ends. Promise?"

"Okay." She looked down, wondering how she was going to break the news to him.

Φ

"You're not like the other girls," he said, pulling her toward him. "You're exciting and unpredictable...I like that, Katherine. Marry me."

Her throat swelled. Was that his news? She had come to tell him she didn't love him. That she was in love with another man. A poet.

"I need to tell you something, Jake."

"Later, later," he whispered in her hair, pulling her into an alcove of an abandoned shop. "First *my* conversation." He caressed her ear with his lips and played them over her neck and face. It sent a shiver through her. She closed her eyes and thought of Vincent: *'with thee conversing I forget all time'*. She let him maneuver her to a dark corner. He kissed her eyelids, her cheeks, her hair. Perhaps she'd been too harsh. He wanted to marry her, after all, to share an ordinary life together.

She helped him shrug out of his clothes and smelled his longing. She let him undress her, pull her down on top of him, taste the hollow of her shoulder, her breasts, her nipples. She imagined Vincent's trembling hands, his tender glance. His fingers exploring, diving into her dark longing for him. She shuddered, surrendering to her passion. *'Flesh of flesh, bone of my bone thy art'*. Later, she thought. Then thought no longer.

Φ

Something nudged Vincent awake. "Katherine is with her lover," said Mildred, peering down at him.

Vincent roused himself, wiped the sleep from his eyes and croaked, "Library, connect with SenTech sensor, subject carrier Jake. On screen." Katherine's face appeared on the huge screen on the far wall. She looked straight at him with longing. Her lips parted as she drew closer. Vincent flung off the covers and sat up, naked, ignoring his misshapen leopard-body. He snatched the V-set from the nightstand and pulled it over his head, letting the translucent screen cover his face. "Library, activate SenTech virtual program. Save this scenario as Katherine Seventeen. Remember to voice-over 'Jake' with 'Vincent'."

The room disappeared, replaced by a dark corridor. He lay on the cold surface of the grimy floor. Her warm body slid over him and he smelled the sweet spice of her desire. Perhaps he could find Eden on Earth after all! He felt himself firm and whispered, *"'Part of my soul I seek thee, Katherine, and claim my other half'."*

She drew back and peered at him with wide eyes. Then she tilted her head, gave him a searching look, and leaned forward. He felt her breath on him. "Vincent?"

His heart soared. *"'How can I live without thee, how forgo thy sweet converse and love so dearly join'd, to live again in these wild woods forlorn'?"*

She stared at him in astonishment, then broke into a wonderful smile and kissed him. She whispered into his hair, *"'With that thy gentle hand seiz'd mine, Vincent, I yielded, and from that time see how beauty is excell'd by manly grace and wisdom, which alone is truly fair'."*

19

Frantic for her, he clasped her and thrust into her moist haven. She gasped. "Oh, Vincent! Vincent!"

His spirit soared like a falcon to her tender loving. When it was over she leaned her cheek against his and murmured, "I love you, Vincent." He closed his eyes. If this were only true, he thought. It felt so real. When he opened his eyes she was staring at him with intense wonder. "You're crying...."

Vincent wrenched off the V-set and blinked the tears from his eyes. The room returned. He was back on his bed. The screen was dark and she was gone. Vincent glanced down at himself, covered in his own semen. He let his eyes flutter shut and clung to her sweet words of love, ignoring what he knew— that her uttering of his name was the computer's doing—and imagined the sweet perfume of her love mingled in his own.

Then he bowed his head and stared at his shriveled hands. They looked like withered twigs, infested with parasites. His body a hideous monstrosity. It was obvious that she loved Jake. How could he ever think she loved him?

He swallowed down his emotion and stumbled to his feet. Clearing his throat, he said, "Please clean up the bed, Mildred. I'll be in the shower."

"Do you wish to save this scenario?" he heard its tinny voice behind him.

"Yes, yes," he growled. This was the only way he could have her. "Tell the library to flag this one with four stars."

Vincent caught his own reflection in the hall mirror and stopped. The stretched skin of his face glistened like plastic that had been meddled with, its integrity destroyed. He pulled at the single tuft of hair on his mottled head and, feeling the pain, stared into his own narrowed eyes in challenge.

The crying, the poetry, were surely *his* feelings and thoughts, not Jake's? Yet Jake had expressed them to Katherine. Up to now Vincent had been convinced that SenTech provided strictly a one-way conduit from carrier to Overseer. SenTech was designed to help Vincent sense everything that occurred to his carrier, but only as an active spectator. What just happened with Katherine implied that Jake had acted on a subliminal message from Vincent. That he, Vincent, *had initiated action.* He blinked at the realization and saw his eyes widen with excitement, then guilt and dread.

What have I started?

Φ

Katherine lay upon Jake, her cheek pressed against his furry chest. She gently stroked his hair. "You were so sweet to quote Milton," she said. "I had no idea you'd taken an interest."

Jake brushed his eyes with his hand and looked baffled. "I'm not sure why—how. It just came out of my mouth. I've never read Milton. You're the one who reads that stuff."

Her lips curled in sudden amusement. She liked seeing him vulnerable. "Perhaps a poetic muse has invaded your mind," she teased and ran her fingers through his curls. He'd shown that beneath his reserve there lay a depth she'd never suspected.

He thought for a moment. "Maybe I *should* start reading it."

She buried her nose in his hair, inhaling his musky smell. "And, the crying—"

He drew back, embarrassed, and shot her a dark look. "Why did you call me Vincent? Who's Vincent?"

"Did I?" Katherine swallowed. When they'd made love, she'd lost herself in his eyes, imagined for a brief moment that he really was Vincent. Spirit and flesh mingled into one whole. She bowed her head. "He's only a character in a virtual game I was playing," she said casually. Vincent could never be really hers. Uncomfortable with her outer beauty, he'd irrevocably isolated his physical self from her. Didn't want her. She'd been sharing "love-notes" with a phantom. But Jake was physically here with her. She could touch him. Could feel his warm breath upon her face.

And he loved her. She knew that now: no man had ever wept for her before. He'd even quoted poetry to her. She decided against breaking it off. Maybe there was a little of Vincent even in Jake.

A Butterfly in Peking

My brother and I cower behind my older cousin as she strides with long steps toward the foreman at the Corporation Farm. The foreman slouches, legs spread apart, atop an ATV with a radio strapped to his head. He oversees several huge vehicles that worm their way across the vast field, tilling and seeding. I fix on his sun burnt belly, distended under a shirt stained with grease and old food. Indolent eyes flicker across us like a scorching flame. "What have we here?" he bellows. "Urchins for dinner?"

I shrink back. Greasy black hair coils like knotted rope to his shoulders. He looks like the Techno my cousin just killed and in sudden panic I wonder if he knows. She raises her chest and tilts her head back proudly. Her face is smeared with dirt and her hair is matted and tangled with leaves from spending the night in the forest. Backlit, her chaotic hair seems to give off its own light, as though it's been dipped in heaven. She says in a clear voice, "Techno vigilantes raided our farm and killed our parents."

The foreman snorts. "Then you must be little Greenies to barbecue on a skewer—"

"We're *children*," she counters. "We have nowhere else to go. If you turn us away you'll be sentencing us to sure death. They don't care who they kill. Please, you must help us." Her hands reach out in supplication. "We work hard and we don't eat much."

The foreman's gaze softens and his gaze sweeps her body, eyes devouring her. She's charmed the beast with her precocious tongue and he takes us into his lair.

Ω

I gaze at the flat horizon that trembles in the blistering heat. The sun beats down on me and the rain-saturated field. The workmen and women have left the shiny beetles slumbering in a neat row as they retire inside. My cousin and I weed the hardpan and my younger brother sweeps the kitchen floor, while they drink in the cool interior of the corporation farm workhouse and complain loudly about the poor conditions. I can hear them from here. Too little food, too much work, they shout. They argue about the revolution. The breeze flings their words in my direction. "You're a God-damned Greenie, Birch. They're destroying our society—"

"They're saving the fucking planet!"

"Oh, yeah? Not until they fuck all of us first!"

"Look around you. We're already fucked. Technos are pissing away this planet—"

Chairs scrape. I brace myself for the inevitable brawl. Other raised voices join in. Soon they will spill out of the barracks, fists flying.

Shielding my eyes from the sun, I watch my cousin dance lightly over the clods of dirt to the cistern outside the kitchen for a drink of water. The flush of heat glows on her face. Ignoring the commotion inside, she waves to me and her smile draws one out from me. A gust of wind blows up from behind, dulling the voices inside. I smell rain. The distant roll of thunder murmurs of a coming storm.

It is her thirteenth birthday today. No one will know, and I wipe the surging pleasure from my mind. There will be no birthday cake. No presents. At least we are alive and safe. That is her present. The revolution, which sweeps the country like a violent storm, carves cities into rubble. It casts families across the landscape like pebbles in a rough sea. It left our parents dead in its wake, made my cousin a killer and us three orphaned itinerants, fleeing here with the hope of shelter.

She raises a cup of water from the cistern to her mouth, then lets it drop and runs into the kitchen. I'm annoyed that she has abandoned me to tend the field alone. The workhouse has grown quiet. Perhaps the workers have all fallen into a drunken stupor. The gusts rise to an open-mouthed roar and sting my eyes with dust. Coal-black clouds chase each other like predators. After a while I walk slowly to the kitchen, shielding my eyes from the flying grit.

Hearing malicious laughter within, I hesitate at the open door then force myself to creep forward. I peer around the threshold then freeze, stiff with fear. My brother huddles, naked, on the floor. His dark clothes lie strewn like dried blood at a slaughter. My cousin writhes against the strong hold of several men. Her face is pale with alarm and her eyes dark with terror. They laugh and rip off her clothes. A large man, naked from the waist down, lurches toward her and growls in a drunken slur, "Here's the witch who convinced our piss-pot foreman to give away our food! Well, here's some dessert for you!" He drives into her, rough and insistent, his grunts to her cries a discordant duet of lust and pain.

Someone points to me. "Look! The other kid!" They all turn. For a brief moment—an eternity—my eyes lock with hers. They plead for my help.

I bolt. Her screams chase me stumbling across the uneven soil, tripping on the ruts, refusing to glance back. My face hits the ground. I scramble up, taste dirt in my mouth, and fight into a gallop. Gulping in air. Ears ringing. Eyes blurred with tears. Nose bleeding.

Run. Stinking son of a bitch. Run. Run.

I've left her there, screaming. And, because I didn't stay to hear the screams end, they never will. I hide, shivering in the forest, as the earth grows black and rain pelts me. The onslaught is over in minutes. It leaves me limp like rotting vegetation as I watch the shafts of sunlight pierce the dark mantle and touch the landscape with an unearthly glow. I inhale the skunky smell of marsh plants and imagine her ravaged body discarded on the rubbish pile like old meat. As the shadows of the afternoon enfold me in their skeletal embrace, I stumble out of my garden of moss and ferns and scuttle over the vast field, hoping no one will see me. I slide into hardpan pools and the wet clay clings to my boots and weighs me down.

When I creep into the kitchen, I find her curled like a wounded deer on the floor where they've left her. My brother lies pressed against her, asleep, and she strokes his whimpering face. I want to embrace her, let her cry in my arms. Instead I turn my head away and stand fixed like a stone, cold and heavy. I cannot gaze into her sunken eyes. They sting my soul.

When she finally raises herself off the floor without my help, she scoops my little brother in her thin arms, takes up her tattered clothes and limps back to the sleeping barracks. She does not look back to see if I'm following.

The days bleed into months and she appears unharmed, looking like she always did, face quietly sanguine and eyes glowing like a warm campfire. But I sense her distance. My little brother clings to her. I avoid them both. When our eyes meet one day, I imagine reproach in hers but know their gaze only reflects my own emptiness. I perceive in that ethereal look that they've molested her and probably my brother several times since.

When I'm not working I crawl and hide under the porch floorboards where the dirt smells acrid and I spy on the workers from inside my dark enclave. I feel cursed in my fortune. Am I successfully evading them or do the bastards leave me alone because they sense my worthlessness? I crouch there and recite poetry like her bedtime stories to us. She is silent now. After kissing my brother on the forehead and wishing me a good night, she slips quietly into her bed. I lie stiff under the moldy covers and listen to her hitched breathing in the bed beside me. I know she's crying herself to sleep.

Now I crouch under the porch with aching knees and recite her favorite poem like a mantra:

To see a world in a grain of sand, and Heaven in a wild flower.
Hold infinity in the palm of your hand and eternity in an hour.
He who binds himself to a joy does the winged life destroy;
He who kisses the joy as it flies lives in eternity's sunrise.

Ω

When the Gaians liberate the Techno Corporation Farm, I return to the new city, which enjoys a peace, disrupted only by the occasional sniper—disgruntled Techno reactionaries who lurk and take pot shots at anyone. My brother returns to his schooling and my cousin and I find a livelihood under the new regime.

I embrace the Green science and after a time become a leader in my field, giving papers at conferences and overseeing an elite cadre of researchers. Feeling secure in my growing prominence, I become daring in my work. I invoke the long abandoned chaos theory and apply it to my models of ecosystem behavior. The signature of chaos appeals to me, how the subtle effect of a single event has the potential to spiral into overwhelming and irrevocable change. Chaoticists call it the Butterfly Effect: sensitive dependence on initial conditions, based on the strange notion that a butterfly stirring the air in Peking today could set off a tornado in Texas next month. I recognize its hand in everything I see—including the behavior of my cousin. I observe how the imperceptible mark of that initial disturbance has with time cascaded into a turbulent squall. As though a wounded bird thrashes, trapped within her, its wings smashing her insides more violently with every breath she draws in.

Seeking obscurity, she finds a position far beneath her capacity as a plant biologist in the Department of Industrial

Ecology and sinks into oblivion. I see little of her, but there is seldom a moment when I do not think of her. While my busy lecture tour rarely gives me time to entertain in my penthouse suite, she languishes in the poor section of town with the bus driver she married and two wild-haired children. Is she happy?

Ω

The day I find the courage to visit her, I feel excited and nervous like a child. I stride toward the D.I.E. building entrance, bubbling with things to share with her. Once inside I see her waiting patiently for me in the large mall. She turns and smiles. It draws one out from me.

A loud report jolts me. She jerks back with an expression of surprise then falls, sprawling unnaturally on the floor as a red flower spreads over her breast. A woman screams and flings her hands to her mouth.

As others chase the sniper, I stand fixed like a cold stone and watch her gasp her last breaths then shiver. Her eyes flicker like a dying flame, then the light in them takes flight and her blank gaze upward is still like a dark pool. My heart beats like a mallet and I ache with a million unfinished sentences.

Ω

I scour the chaos for those fragments of memory, taped together by longing, and see her as she once was, as she always was. She was my beautiful cousin, and when we were still children, she killed for us. Using the hunting bow her father gave her, she slew a man who charged at us with a knife, the same one he'd used to kill our parents. When my brother was attacked, she flew to his aid and threw herself into a den of assault. Then, when she pleaded for my help, I ran away.

I was just a boy, only ten years old. Now I know better. The revolution defined what I am. She faced fear head on, bravely pushed it aside and rose to the call. I let fear chase me away.

Now, I wander dark shores, stranded in that moment of agony, still hearing her screams.

Aching to fly.

Angel's Promises

Rebecca stared through the window to where the sun trembled on the horizon and inflamed the sky. She contrasted what she saw with the dark inner-city, dank with despair, from which they'd retrieved him. Pacing her outer-city office like a trapped panther, she fidgeted with her dress and raked her dark hair back with her fingers. She strained to hear footsteps approaching and felt her heart race with—what? What did she feel? Exhilaration? Terror? A terse rap at the door was her only warning before it swung open and the face she had not seen in four years stared boldly at her. The fire in his coal-black eyes stirred up memories of when she'd met him, kissed him and deserted him.

~ 1 ~

Belly aching with hunger, Rebecca glanced down at Isabelle huddled next to her in the gutted apartment that was once home. It was four days since they'd lost their mother in the crowded mall. Rebecca listened to the murmurs of the city in her head: a low hush mingled with the stirrings of cryptic metallic sounds, chopped up words, bleeps and sighs. Like a million voices in the distance, they came and went like the ebbing and swelling surf of the sea. She no longer mentioned the sounds to Isabelle, who could not hear them, because it frightened her too much.

Rebecca had heard a rumor that the outer-city was searching for people who could interface with AIs. They called them veemelds. Could she be one? As much as she wished to return, she refused to leave her little sister behind. Nothing would ever separate them, she thought, glancing down at Isabelle's urchin face. She'd promised.

Rebecca's gaze swept the place. Some vagrant had vandalized and torched it. Nothing of theirs remained, not that there was much to begin with. She rose and wandered into what used to be their bedroom, Isabelle scrambling behind. Black and sodden, it reeked of kerosene and urine. Her gaze rested on her old bed, torn and stained, where her mother used to awaken her every night, smelling of whiskey, then crawl in beside her, clutch Rebecca to her breast and sob.

Rebecca turned abruptly from the gutted bedroom and said, "We have to go now." She was fifteen and could take care of herself and her twelve-year old sister if she had to.

Isabelle scrambled behind. "Can't we go back to the outer-city and visit Uncle Carl till mummy comes back?"

She isn't coming back, Rebecca thought. She rolled her eyes and shook her head at her sister. "And how'd we get there, you silly? On wings?" As if they could simply climb out of the dark depths of the inner-city. Besides, Uncle Carl was mean. He'd said that anyone who ended up techno-slaving for the inner-city AIs deserved their fate. There'd been no choice for her mother who'd lost her wits after their father was taken away. Rebecca pushed out her lower lip and narrowed her eyes at the thought of Uncle Carl's stern face. Seeing the tears stream down Isabelle's cheeks, Rebecca took her hand. "Never mind, Izzy. I'll take care of you."

They headed to the mall, hoping to find some scraps of food. They staked out a Food Stop and patience finally paid off when a woman got up with a half-eaten oatcake. The girls followed her to a waste bin and watched her drop the cake into the bin. After a quick glance around, Rebecca dove in after it but a dirty hand snatched the cake first. Rebecca jerked up and gazed into a filthy face.

31

"Th-th-this is *my* bin," stammered the boy. He was about her age and stared at her with intense slag-black eyes. Blinking through dark strands of hair, he stroked his long face, smeared with dirt and grease. Then he flicked back his shoulder-length hair and studied the two girls with a smirk that unsettled Rebecca. "You t-t-techno-slummers?"

She'd heard of them. They were orphans of the inner-city, waste products of desperate and over-indulgent techno-slaves. And troublemakers for the AIs. Vermin, who choked up the cyber-system, disturbed their complacent humming, stole into their metal bellies and snuck off with their secrets. "We're looking for my mother," Rebecca replied, curbing a frown.

"That's what they all s-s-say, after their parents ab-b-bandon them," he said as though he was discussing a school event. He smacked his lips as he chewed. "She's b-been gone awhile," he said with a full mouth. "I can tell."

Isabelle puckered her face, ready to cry.

"Here." He broke off a piece of the oatcake and handed it to Isabelle. "You can share my bin until you get one of your own," he stuttered, offering Rebecca a piece. "We're family. We look after each other, especially from the cypols. I'm Neo." He puffed up his chest and tilted his head back proudly. "You probably heard about the mess I caused in the Food-Center. I got us twenty kilos of nano-soup."

Rebecca refused the piece of oat cake, even though Isabelle had already accepted hers and was gratefully eating. "I told you, we're not techno-slummers," she said in a huff. "We're just waiting for our mother to come back."

"Yeah, like when chaos turns to order."

~ 2 ~

"What d'ya mean they talk?" Neo squatted next to Rebecca in the cramped makeshift shack, as they repaired a computer built with some scrap parts they'd found. He dug his dirty nails into his tangled hair and squinted at her.

"Can't you hear them too, Neo?" Rebecca said in a faltering voice. She shifted her weight from one knee to the other, suddenly giddy under his penetrating stare. She caught his scent, sharp with old sweat, felt her face heat and fought down the confusing storm that surged through her abdomen. Lately she'd caught him studying her with such intensity that it made her blush. His opinion meant more to her than anything.

Neo tilted his head to one side. "You making this up?" His name wasn't really Neo. It was Colin Baker, but he'd abandoned it like the parents who'd given him the name had abandoned him. All the techno-slummers had given themselves new names. She'd chosen Angel, the nickname her father gave her. "Machines don't talk to people, Angel," Neo said, shaking his head at her. He stood up. "I gotta get some quantum couplers." He studied her for a moment. "Get a grip, Angel. You're still looking for your mother a year after she abandoned you! A cypol probably caught her and she's been recycled into something by now, maybe the nano-soup you ate today."

She thought him cruel to have said that. Mocking the promise she'd made to her father the day he was arrested. He'd turned at the threshold, flanked by two policemen as her mother and sister wailed uncontrollably and Rebecca stood brave like a soldier: *Take care of your mother and sister for me, till I return, Angel …I will, father, I promise….*He never did return, of course. They'd accused him of being a luddite —she didn't know what that was —and she never saw him again.

Several of the younger orphans had gathered around in the small bivouac built from scrap parts cemented with the detritus of urban fast living. Rebecca clenched her fists and worked her jaw as she watched Neo brush past the giggling children. Letting her anger subside in silence, she decided that from then on she would avoid confiding in him. It was too painful.

But that night, when the little children lay asleep in their nests of garbage and she listened with her eyes closed to the droning throb of the machines in her head, Neo startled her by touching her shoulder. Her eyes darted open to his reckless smile and her face smoldered with the thought that he meant to kiss her. But he was only excited about her strange talent and what it meant for them all. She inhaled his smoky metal scent and controlled her breathing as he shared his plan, totally unaware of the effect he was having on her.

That was when they began to invade the cyber world of the inner-city to feed and clothe themselves. Although she disagreed with stealing, Rebecca sensed that her ability to tap into the AI world not only fed her undernourished companions, but also bolstered their morale. What else could she do? They were starving, cold and sick. And they had no one they could go to. Turning themselves in to the Care-Center facility was not an option. They'd heard horror stories of what went on there. No one ever came back once they went in. Nano-soup.

~ 3 ~

"Cypols!" Neo shouted. His voice rang in the mall, empty now in the deep of the night. Rebecca looked up from the public computer she'd hacked into and her gaze followed Neo's to where a shrill whine grew louder. Several great metal birds of prey swooped down, their burnished wings glinting as they selected their targets and homed in. The children scattered and ran for cover among the garbage and rubble. Isabelle stood stiff with fear.

Rebecca spotted one heading straight for them and leapt to her feet. "Izzy, come on!" She seized Isabelle's hand and ran. Isabelle stumbled behind her, panting. Rebecca tugged her hard, galloping toward a makeshift lean-to. Isabelle gasped and tripped in the rubble. Their hands flew apart. Rebecca dove under cover, expecting Isabelle to be right behind her.

"Becky!" Isabelle shrieked. Rebecca turned and saw the metal bird seize Isabelle with its claws. Her arms flailed out to Rebecca. "Help!" Within a moment Isabelle sailed up, clutched firmly in the great bird's talons as Rebecca, crouched under the corrugated metal, stared in frozen silence. Her sister's wails subsided and she disappeared into the darkness above.

~ 4 ~

Neo's face grew red and blotchy. Rebecca had just told him that she intended to let herself get caught by a cypol.

They were fashioning a table out of an old building support and he reeled away, letting the piece he held fall to the floor. She flinched as the table crashed. "Damn you, Angel!" He spun around to face her, raking his fingers through his long greasy hair. "What about your mother? You going to abandon your search for her? Just like that?"

Rebecca set down the makeshift hammer then straightened up, wiping her hands on her rags. "You're the one who keeps telling me it's useless to keep looking for her. It's been close to two years now." She tilted her head at him and said tartly, "Nano-soup, remember?"

His eyes flashed. "What about your promise?"

Her face heated with defensive anger. "Which one? I promised I'd look after my sister too."

He pouted and his voice dropped to a whisper. "What about our dream…."

It was a wild dream they shared: escape to the outer-city, where the sun shone and the air was fresh from a breeze rich with the wild scent of flowers. Where people walked with unrestrained laughter and AIs only served a limited function as tools, not lords of techno-slaves. She'd corrupted him with her tales of the outer-city and regretted it now. Sold him on a dream that she couldn't deliver.

He waved his gangly arms. "Damn you!" he lashed out. "We're fa-fa-family and you're g-g-going to leave us to rot and s-s-starve." His stammer was worse than usual. It got that way when he was upset.

She stiffened. "You were around long before I arrived. Besides, Neo, you can do most of what I can do. It's not like you *need* me—"

"I can't talk to the machines—"

Rebecca stomped her foot in frustration and stalked forward until they stood facing one another less than a meter apart. "Neither can I, Neo. I told you, I can't talk to them, only hear them."

"It's the same thing!"

"No it isn't!"

They were both panting, eyes blazing in stalemate. His breath reeked of nano-soup. She let her shoulders slump and looked away with a sigh. She knew he was only hiding his pain under this tirade. She would miss him too, more than she cared to admit.

Neo hunched over and sobbed, "D-d-don't leave me, Angel." The hand that never asked for help thrashed out, like the broken wing of a bird, flopping on the ground.

Overcome by his clumsy supplication, she took his hand. Then she leaned forward and kissed him lightly on the lips. Stunned, his eyes widened. She savored his delicious vulnerability like the nectar of a flower unfolding as he opened to her kiss, his mouth wrapping itself around it. When she withdrew from him, he leaned with her, reluctant to separate. He fumbled for her, clutched her tightly and laid his cheek upon her breast. She stroked his head, smelling his unwashed hair, and felt him shake with silent sobs. Her eyes heated with tears. She fought the confusion between the craving to stay and the need to help her sister. She'd promised, after all. "I'll come back for you," she said in a trembling voice. "I won't leave you behind. I promise."

~ 5 ~

As the rest of the techno-slummers dashed for cover,

Rebecca stood fixed. Her heart pounded as she listened to the familiar squeal of the approaching cypol. Neo lunged for her, tugging hard. Determined, she fought him off and thought down the panic surging inside: I'm going to do it this time. I'm going to let it catch me.

"Damn you, Angel!" Neo screamed. "And damn your promises!" He dashed to safety.

She swallowed down her fear and curbed the instinct to hunker and flee. She could see the cypol's gleaming eyes. Saw it veer toward her. Lock on her. There was no escape now. She'd be joining her sister soon. It had been a week since the cypol took Isabelle. What if she was dead? What if the cypols just took you up to their lair in the darkness of the ceilings and devoured you, like Neo said? What if her sacrifice was for nothing, wouldn't reunite her with Isabelle but would simply put an end to her life?

Rebecca ran. But the cypol was almost upon her. *You will not be hurt*, it seemed to say. Did she imagine it? Stunned, Rebecca broke from her run, let her body go limp as the cypol scooped her up. The air rushed across her face as she soared up and felt exhilaration. I'm coming, Isabelle, she thought. I'm coming to save you. She glimpsed Neo staring up from the shadows, his face twisted in anguish, as she approached the rafters. Trembling with the memory of their first kiss, she whispered in a hoarse voice, "I'll come back, Neo. I promise."

A doorway opened into a yawning darkness. The bird sailed through and she was enveloped by pitch black. Her heart raced and she caught an overly sweet, almost cloying smell as she grew weary and fell into a deep slumber.

Rebecca awoke groggily to loud voices in her head. It was still dark. She lay bound with her back on a smooth, hard surface.

She recognized the metal voices as their AI rulers. *She's definitely a veemeld,* said one. *Go fetch Christian from the outer-city.*

We can sell this one.

Another said, *Look at this, Alpha. Her V29 prostaglandins appear abnormally high. Even for a veemeld. What can it mean?*

Perhaps we should charge a higher price. It is a sweet deal, Omega. We rid ourselves of these pests and the outer-city humans pay us for them. They use our waste to interface with their primitive AIs to run their disorganized outer-city. Beats recycling. Reuse, when you can, I always say. This one will fetch us a good price . . .

She strained to hear more but the voices faded and she lost herself in the dark void. When she regained consciousness, she heard more voices, this time not in her head. They were exchanged in mild argument and one of them was definitely human.

"—You know we want her, damn it!" the human, an older male, said in frustration.

"Only if you pay double the price, Christian," a shrill metal voice insisted.

"All right, all right," the human conceded wearily. "Are there more like her?"

"Doesn't she have a sister?" rejoined a tin voice. "I think we picked her up earlier."

Another metal voice cut in, "She tested negative. Not a veemeld. We disposed of her. She's been recycled."

No! Not Isabelle! She pulled frantically on the bindings and squeezed her eyes tight to the tears that filled them. Oh, God, no! Not my baby sister...

The voices continued, oblivious to her pain. " The girl has an uncle in the outer city. Carl Douglas," Christian said.

No! Not there! Let me stay here with Neo.

"...I'll contact the uncle and arrange for her departure within the hour."

No! Rebecca screamed out but no sound emerged. The weariness overcame her. Oh, Neo. I've left you for nothing. Our dream. So many promises to keep. So many promises....

~6~

He'd cut his dark hair short and his face had matured. A few stubborn locks fell over his temple. Full lips, held tightly, were poised on a rugged and unshaven jaw. She appraised his torso, visible beneath his tattered rags. Now twenty-one, he'd filled out from his awkward adolescence into a man's shape, tall and strongly muscled. She hardly recognized him, except for those intense coal-black eyes.

Rebecca pointed to a chair facing her desk. "Please," and slid into the chair behind her desk. She placed her hands flat, caressing the smooth wood.

Refusing to approach, he planted his legs apart and crossed his arms over his chest. His eyes narrowed with suspicion. "Why'd you bring me here?" he said without a trace of a stammer. He's learned control, she thought. Become a warrior poet. "Why didn't the AIs kill me?" he challenged. "I'm not a veemeld. I'm no use to you people."

Could it be that he didn't recognize her? Trying to control the emotion in her voice she said, "Neo, it's me...Angel."

His face paled. A tide of astonishment swept the dark hostility aside and his arms dropped to his side like lead. "A-a-ngel?" he stammered. Then anger boiled up. It fired his eyes with rage and he charged toward her. She recoiled in alarm. But he stopped at her expression and a miserable smile crossed his lips. She watched him take in a deep breath before speaking with more control, "I was right. When the human slaves are no longer useful like your drunk mother, the AIs recycle them." His mouth curled into a self-mocking smirk. "Nano-soup." He appraised her wearily and pursed his lips. The expression in his eyes opened to his pain and she heard the agony break over his voice. "I thought you were dead, Rebecca."

She flinched at his use of her proper name and swallowed.

"Couldn't eat nano-soup after that." Then he veiled his anguish with disgust. "But eventually news filtered down that the outer-city had a new veemeld with special powers, she could hear the machines in her head." He sneered. "And I knew you were alive." He flicked his hand to dismiss all his previous pain as if it were unimportant. "You probably knew you'd be safe and fetch a good price too. Not brave like I'd thought, more like self-serving."

"It wasn't like that, Neo," she said in a trembling voice.

His eyes gleamed with open hatred. "I really believed you. I believed all the things you said about escaping and living here together, but you never really meant it, did you?"

"Neo—"

"Once you got here, you forgot all about us."

By *us* he meant *him*. Did that tremulous first kiss taste bitter to him now?

"And I can see why." His accusing gaze slid from her face and roamed her plush office. His eyes rested on the blazing sky. She heard a tremor in his voice, "You got what you wanted." He glared at the plaques of distinction and achievement that hung on her wall. Then his head snapped at her with a scowl. "Chaos knows why I'm here now. Was it a glitch? Some embarrassing mistake you have to fix? You certainly didn't earn your excellent reputation by thinking of us or our welfare."

Shivering with anger, she found her voice, "Do you think that was my choice?" Propelled to her feet, she gripped the desk and locked her eyes on his. "They—my uncle—kept me from going back to look for you. I was trapped here in a paradise without a heart. It was our dream and my thoughts of you..." and that sweet kiss "...that kept me from drowning in despair.

40

Kept me afloat these past four years with the hope that you hadn't been caught and recycled like my sister. I realized that the only way I was going to find you and bring you out was if I played along and became the best veemeld the outer-city had. My prize was that I eventually had a chance to talk to the AIs in the inner-city and convinced them to sell you to me." She swallowed the emotion rising in her throat and tried to gauge his intense look. Was he still angry with her? She couldn't blame him. Feeling utter defeat, she forced the last words past a tide of anguish, "I thought I would never find you." Her eyes heated with tears and his face blurred in pools of dismay. "And now that I have, it's only to find out that I destroyed our dream. I lost you anyway." Unable to meet his fierce eyes her gaze dropped to the floor and her voice fell like petals from a wilted flower. "I've broken all my promises."

"No you haven't," he said in a gentle voice that drew her gaze. With a few strides he'd closed the distance between them and stood so close to her, she could feel his breath upon her. His smoky metal scent coiled around her in a heady embrace as he placed his hands on her shoulders and leaned forward. His icy glare had melted to dark pools of warmth. "You didn't break the one you made to me, Angel, when you first kissed me."

She trembled as he took her face in his hands. Then his lips were on hers and she felt like they'd never been apart, tasting the mature fruit of his love. He took her in his arms as though he never meant to let her go and she finally felt like she was home.

She thought of her mother and sister, recycled in the inner-city, feeding into that eternal cycle of altering form…nano-soup…the cell of a beating heart…the suspended dust upon which bloomed the blushing sky. As she gazed into Neo's midnight eyes, now reflecting the glow of sunset, Rebecca realized that he'd just given her the key to her legacy of promises. Every promise she'd made was a declaration to nurture a tender seed.

The rest was up to God.

Frames

The ruins of the city rippled in the heat like a bad movie. Gunther raked his fingers through his hair and paced the exposed second floor of the dilapidated building. His gaze panned the city. Haze the color of rust lingered over phantom pools on the horizon.

"It's hot as hell," he complained, shrugging his Computerized Automatic Rifle over his shoulder. His camouflage fatigues clung to his body like something he needed to shed. "I'm dying in this heat." Several flies buzzed around his head and he flapped his gangly arm madly in the air. "Damn flies."

Slouched against some rubble, Rick ignored him. He ran diagnostics on the CARifle stretched out on his lap, verifying the output data on his eye-com. Rick's sullen face was barely visible under the vee-set strapped to his head. Gunther pulled out a stick of gum, unraveled the wrapper and pushed the wad into his mouth. Smacking his lips, he savored the mint flavor and tossed the wrapper.

"Asshole!" Rick snapped. "Pick that up."

Gunther snatched the wrapper. The rifle slipped off his shoulder and clattered to the ground. Forcing on a nervous grin he scrambled to pick up the weapon then stepped on the vee-set he'd yanked off earlier.

"We're Gaians." Rick's finger stabbed the green band on his arm. "Protectors of the Earth, asshole." He turned back to his CARifle and muttered, "Just like a filthy Techno...no idea why you're doing anything...."

Gunther replaced the vee-set on his head and slung the CARifle over his shoulder. He sagged under its weight and let his gaze stray to where the roof had been blasted away. The air smelled of smoke and burning metal. He blinked away the sweat that ran into his eyes and squinted at the sun, suspended in a yellow dust cloud. "Those lousy Technos caused this heat wave. We're turning into a desert!"

Rick ignored him and kept tinkering with his weapon.

"Hell, if it weren't for this revolution," Gunther continued, "the planet would be toast already...." He trailed, lost for a moment in a terrifying place. More flies buzzed furiously around his head. "Get off!" he shouted and shook his head violently. He frowned and muttered, "We better see some action soon." Gunther poked the rubble with his rifle. "When I took this post I was glad I'd be toasting any coward Technos trying to escape the city." He raised his rifle, aimed at an imaginary target and made clicking sounds with his tongue. "When I asked the Gaian committee for this post—"

"Asshole!" Rick spat. "You didn't ask for it; they assigned you."

Gunther half-grinned, exposing dirty teeth, and shrugged.

Rick spit on the ground. "I know your story, turd. You hid in some hole during the whole clone siege. Waiting to find out who won so you could take their side."

Gunther inhaled the gum and coughed.

Rick sneered. "I figure they put you with me to keep an eye on you. Make sure you don't run away like them other Technos." He rubbed the graying stubble on his creased face and his eyes narrowed to slits. "Hell, you were probably a Techno before we found you. Come to mind, you look like one of them..."

44

Gunther's heart pounded. He followed Rick's gaze to his own smooth hands then glanced toward the outskirts of town and felt his throat swell. He thought of the Techno shop he worked in until that man with the horse-face came and asked him all those questions about his sister, insinuating that she was leading a Gaian underground: which she was. Shivering inside, Gunther said in a hollow voice, "Techno clones murdered my sister. I could kill—"

"You could never kill anyone, asshole. And how is it that *you* got away, huh?" Rick raised his brows.

Face burning, Gunther stroked his rifle with short nervous motions. Rick made a scoffing sound and returned to his diagnostics. Gunther swallowed, wondering if he was going to vomit. He forced down the intrusive nightmare: his sister being bludgeoned to death in her city-center apartment the night the horse-faced man had questioned him. Gunther had been too frightened to even warn her. Instead he'd sat in the silence of his apartment, hands poised over the vee-caller, and watched the lights of the city strobe like an old movie reel across his wall. Early the next morning, a friend of Kelly's veed Gunther with the news and he fled to the streets, afraid to return to the shop or to his apartment. He hid in Metro Park and watched Techno clones, half-human and half-machine, raid house after house. Then one night the Gaians bombed the Metro Tower Complex, knocking the lights out of the city—and him. Some Gaian had found him passed out among some rubble and now he was with Rick. Gunther blurted, "Didn't you lose family?"

"My family are the Gaians. So are yours, asshole. Remember that." Rick checked his vee-set and pushed himself off the ground. "Let's grab a bite. No one's coming now in the middle of the day."

Gunther nodded, trying to smile. The thought of food revolted him. As he turned, Gunther spotted a man, woman and child on the street below, furtively making their way toward them. "Hey! Look!" he pointed, gulping in air and chest heaving.

"Where the hell did they find time to have a kid in all this?" Rick snarled. "We should shoot them all."

"Yeah! We should!" Gunther cried in a shrill voice between racing shallow breaths.

"You talk too much," Rick said. He checked the setting on his rifle. "Let's go."

They scrambled down from their perch and dropped in front of the three travelers. The woman shrieked and gathered up the whimpering three-year old who buried his face in her chest. She was young, about Gunther's age, and might have been pretty, except her dirty hair hung in a tangled mat over a face gaunt from lack of food. Avoiding those saucer eyes that stared at him from cavernous pits, his gaze slid to the scrawny man. The man cast his eyes down and shoved his hands in his pockets.

"Where d'you think you're going?" Rick challenged, pointing his rifle at them. "You know there's a curfew. No one's allowed in or out of the city."

"But we're not Technos," the man stammered. His eyes darted from the green band on Gunther's arm to Rick's rifle.

"You're either with the Gaians saving the planet or with the Technos who're destroying it," Rick said. "There's no in-between, asshole."

Sensing her husband's hesitation, the woman straightened up. "Our child's so young," she said in a quivering voice, her gaze darting between Rick and Gunther. "He's starving here, in the city. He doesn't know anything about revolution or war. We have friends in the country who can feed him. Surely you can take pity on him and let us go. We can't be any use to you burdened with him—"

Gunther flinched at the gunshot.

The impact tore the boy from her arms and splattered her face with blood. Gunther's gaze lurched from Rick's CARifle to the child sailing to the pavement as the mother reeled backwards. She scrambled to the dead boy and fell to her knees.

"Liam!" she wailed, scooping up the limp body and clutching it to her breast, rocking. "My baby!"

"Oh, God! Oh, God!" The man danced nervously around his sobbing wife.

"Shut up!" Gunther shrieked, shivering with adrenaline. He forced down the vile fluid that wanted to come up. "Shut the fuck up!" He stabbed the air repeatedly with his rifle.

"Now, go back and do your duty for the planet," said Rick with icy calmness. "Or I'll have to shoot you too."

The man seized his wife but she refused to get up. Her chest glistened with blood as she clutched the dead child and rocked in a kind of stupor, moaning. He yanked her to her feet with violent force. "Sylvia! Come on!" After a terrified glance at Rick, the man pulled her like a puppet down the street.

Releasing a frantic energy, Gunther sent a stutter of shots around them. "Faster, Technos! Faster!" His gaze darted fearfully to his brooding colleague. Then he laughed hysterically when one of his shots caught the man in the shoulder. The man twitched, stumbled briefly then ran on. "Th-that'll teach 'em," Gunther stammered, watching their figures ripple in the distance, and avoided a glance down at the dark pool of blood, already shimmering with flies. His ears rang in the crushing silence. Until the flies swarmed around his head again, buzzing like a bad channel-connection.

Ψ

"Get over here, asshole!" Rick hissed from behind a pile of mortar and brick. Gunther scrambled over to Rick, hunching up his shoulder to keep his rifle from falling off. He dove next to Rick and peered over the top. What he saw made him shiver. Seven large figures marched toward them in V-formation, brash steps clanking in unison, burnished skulls glaring in the heat.

Gunther fixed his stare on the leader, whose binocular eyes protruded over pale cheeks. A metal snake slithered across his left cheek, molded to his translucent skin, and slid into the corner of his mouth. Gunther's eyes darted to the clone's left arm. All metal and smoke, it glinted menacingly. He was half-human, half-metal. A Techno clone.

"Shit," Rick whispered in a hoarse voice that betrayed fear. "I thought we got them all." He unclipped the lock trigger to his CARifle with shaking hands and adjusted the eye-com of his vee-set. Gunther saw fierce determination supplant the fear in the old man's eyes. "They're not taking me before I get a few of the assholes first." His eyes narrowed as he aimed.

Gunther's heart pounded and he shrank down, trying to make himself as small as possible. Rick's rifle squealed. The leader jerked back and fell. The rest of the clones scattered. Rick sprang up. "Cover me!" he shouted. Shots screamed out of his rifle as he darted after the fleeing cyborgs. "Bastards! You killed my planet!"

Gunther watched two more of them fall, before a clone's shot caught Rick. He twitched, spun and fell. The vee-set flew off his head and his CARifle clattered meters in front of him. A cloud of dust rose around his twisted body as Rick groped for the rifle. "Cover me, asshole!" he snarled. Gunther trembled behind his hideout, stiff with fear.

The four remaining clones cocked their weapons and crept toward Rick's squirming body.

"Gunther! You asshole!" Rick wheezed. A clone stepped on his outstretched arm. Rick's head jerked up. The Techno aimed and shot. Rick's head—what was left of it—fell back. The clone stepped over Rick's body and looked straight at Gunther.

Alarm pounded in his head. Gunther shrank down and pressed his shivering body against the bricks until it hurt.

He heard steps crunching on the rubble. Fear shook him like a vile wind and he wet his pants. He squeezed his eyes shut and heard the shots scream like a tortured woman over his head. The bricks cracked and pinged, spitting grit into his face. Something large thudded beside him. His ears rang in the silence that followed. One eye squinted open and he saw the clone lying next to him.

Something sprang onto the rubble pile above him. Gunther gasped at the slim warrior with a cyborg face. Then the warrior pulled off the vee-set, and a thick mane of dark brown hair tumbled down around the face of an angel. She leaned forward to touch his shoulders gently. "It's okay, soldier," she assured him in a liquid-honey voice. "I'm a Gaian. You're safe. I got them all." He saw the green Gaian arm band on her left arm for the first time. "I'm sorry I arrived too late to help your partner." She bent on one knee to check him for injuries. "I'm Wanda. You don't look hurt. We'll have you back on duty in no time."

His throat closed and everything shut off.

Ψ

Gunther and Wanda picked their way carefully down a side street strewn with chunks of brick and mortar, glass fragments and garbage. Shrugging to keep his CARifle slung over his shoulder, Gunther adjusted the vee-set on his head and glanced anxiously behind him. The cloying stink of diesel fuel and decaying food made him feel sick. Flies buzzed around his head, making him twitch.

Wanda rolled her eyes. "You're not getting squirmy on me again, are you?"

He forced a smile and hung his head. She had insisted that he join her patrol. He wondered if it had been to protect him or to set him straight. He envied Wanda's drive and courage. He stole a glance along her lithe form, somehow still attractive even in camouflaged fatigues, and bright green arm-band tied to her left arm. He guessed she was about his age—twenty-five—but she seemed much older, more sure of herself. He focused on her full lips, held firmly in reproach. The vee-set hid part of her face. Beauty and machine-beast. She didn't seem to have a problem embracing the Techno's tools to fight a war against Techno-technology.

"We're just going to blow away a new hideout where Technos are building vee-coms," Wanda said. That simple.

Gunther frowned. "Something about this makes me feel creepy," he admitted. "What if the tip we got is wrong? What if it isn't a hideout, and this is an ambush?"

"They aren't that organized. It's not like there's any government left. Why do you even think like that?"

"But they say the Technos are building a new army too. Some say they've created a new set of clones even better than the last ones."

Wanda rolled her eyes. "Those clones I saved you from are original models, Gunther. There are no new ones. You've got a bad attitude. We destroyed all their big labs and shops. They can't make more clones," she said. "There's just a few of the old ones left, like the ones you had a run in with last week."

He shrugged and tried to hide the worry on his face.

Her expression softened. "Oh, Gunther," she sighed, reminding him of his older sister. She hadn't seen it coming until it was too late either. They were sitting ducks. He glanced at the green band brandished on his left arm. Technos lurked behind every corner, just waiting for him. He was advertising himself with the stupid thing: here I am. Come and get me! As for the vee-sets and eye-coms and fancy CARifles—Hell, it was all Techno-equipment. Some of it he'd even helped put together. What a joke!

"Wanda, how do you know you're on the right side?"

She halted and turned, now looking really ticked off. "Listen, Gunther." She planted her long legs apart and gazed at him sternly. "You can't spend your days being afraid of death, wondering who's going to win." She shook her head. "You can't choose how you die, but you can choose how you live, Gunther. That's what you take with you."

She sounded just like his sister. Kelly always knew what she wanted. She'd been so sure about her choice to fight against the Technos. He remembered her railing at him about his own indecision. "Gunther, make up your mind," he still heard Kelly's soft voice, "then live by it." Or die by it, Sis. He squinted and shrugged.

Sighting the house, Wanda began to walk briskly. "Come on," she said. "Lets get in there and blow away that filthy Techno hole for Gaia."

Gunther scrambled after her, not wanting to be left behind.

Wanda slid to a window with fluid elegance and lobbed a gas bomb. It smashed the glass and exploded inside. A noxious blue gas billowed out of the window. Wanda and Gunther unslung their rifles, raced to the door and waited. Gunther's heart pounded. He broke into a sweat. This was the part he hated.

The door flew open and a family emerged, coughing and groping with tearful eyes. First a man, then a woman, herding out two young children. Aside from her eyes widening with surprise Wanda didn't hesitate: she opened fire, catching them all before they had a chance to scream or bolt for safety or use the weapons clutched in their hands—even the kids. Careful not to look anyone in the eyes, Gunther winced as he fired. His CARifle punched gaping holes into what he knew was already a dead man.

Wanda sprinted past the bodies and disappeared inside for a few terrifying moments. She emerged in a rush and pointed ahead for him to follow. Gunther sprang after her as she pounded down the stairs without a second look at the sprawled mass of bodies and threw herself behind a pile of rubble. The building exploded. Grit and dust flew out like a spouting volcano. Wanda got up and wiped her hands on her fatigues, coughing in the thick dust. Her face glowered. "Those bastards are even using kids now. They make me sick."

Still, she hadn't hesitated to shoot them, Gunther thought.

"Kids with guns," she said, disgusted. "God, what'll they do next?" She turned and strode toward the alley that would take them home, Gunther scrambling behind her.

Gunther stopped shaking once they rounded a corner of the long alley, where the sweet pungent smell of rotting food and burning metal was welcome. She'd taken him back to firm Gaian territory. Wanda turned to him with a casual smile. "Do you think the Gaians will hold elections the first year?" She obviously intended to set him at ease.

Gunther began to relax. "I don't know—"

A sharp tug on his left arm jerked him off his feet. A gun shot rang. His arm exploded with pain. Tears sprang to his eyes and he felt sick as he fell.

Wanda crouched instantly and swung her rifle in the direction of the sound of the blast. Gunther saw her take a sighting on a nearby building through her eye-com, aim and shoot twice. A figure toppled. It sailed down the twenty-story building and thudded meters away. Gunther saw his white arm band: a Techno sniper.

Wanda scrambled to Gunther and bent over him. Her face softened with concern. He followed her gaze to where his arm was bleeding profusely. It was torn apart at the elbow and the lower arm lay in an unnatural position. His head rang with panic. "It hurts, Wanda."

"I know," she said, touching him gently. Urgent again, "Stay still. I'll put pressure on the wound with..." she looked around frantically, "this," and untied her green arm band. He grimaced with pain while she tied it on his gaping wound as tightly as possible. It wasn't enough. The blood continued to seep out. Wanda dashed to the destroyed figure of the Techno sniper, removed his white arm band and returned to Gunther. Blood had soaked both green arm bands, turning them black. She tied the white arm band as tightly as possible, well above the wound. It seemed to work as a tourniquet.

"Come on," she commanded. "I'll help you back. You'll have to walk, Gunther." She hoisted him up using his good arm. He stumbled to his feet and passed out briefly. When he came to, she was dragging him down the alley. He forced his wobbly legs to keep up with her pace. "Good." She nodded, panting as she bore most of his weight. "Not much farther and we'll be there. You can do it, Gunther."

He focused on her lips, drawn back and moist with effort, and knew that he would follow her wherever she went.

They emerged into Hanging Square. An angry Gaian mob thronged around a makeshift scaffold and shouted obscenities at the body of a Techno partisan swinging slowly on the rope. A girl at the edge of the crowd called above the general raucous. "Look!" she pointed to Wanda and Gunther. "More Technos!"

Gunther glanced from the girl to the white Techno band on his arm. His stomach lurched.

The crowd rushed them like a violent storm. Wanda dropped Gunther and he collapsed to the ground. He expected her to pelt out of there to safety but she stayed with him and swung her rifle up. "We're not Technos!" she screamed. "We're—"

The wave hit. Someone struck her. The rifle fell and she tottered. The crowd held her up. They tore off her vee-set and smashed her face. She went limp but they kept beating her.

His body clenched like an insect pinned against a wall, watching them beat Wanda in staccato.

A dark silhouette obliterated the glaring sun overhead. A shovel, brandished high, swung down as if in slow motion. When it struck his face, it only stung for a moment. He saw himself collapse into an empty husk. It grew thick with flies, sissing like static and filling the darkness of his mouth, his nose, his brain.

He scrambled in a panic for a clear image, but the picture faded away.

Julia's Gift

I inhale deeply to savor the freshness of the air and raise my face to the bright sun bathing in an azure sky. I begin to climb the stairs, averting my eyes from the thousands of people watching me. I falter and nearly stumble as my thoughts sink like a stone in water to Julia and what she did: to that black day twenty-nine years ago when her actions determined who lived and who died, and to the day much later when she ended the curse she'd placed on herself as a result.

Why did she do any of it? Maybe it was because she was the middle child in our family. Psychologists like to say that the middle child acts like an immobile bridge between roles of leadership and childish irresponsibility. Able to see both sides of an argument, they usually make good diplomats, but falter when faced with spontaneous decisions. Like a fish out of water forced to breathe air, Julia gulped in leadership against her nature…and destroyed herself.

How different the course of events might have been if she hadn't acted so boldly that spring day twenty-nine years ago. Would I be here, walking up these steps now? Would Simon have survived? Would Julia still have jumped in front of the tube-jet seventeen years ago? Or would we all have died along with our parents that spring day?

α

The blood-red dawn promised a warm day in April. By mid-morning the smell of Montreal had dissipated. The sun felt like a heat lamp on my face as I stepped outside the farmhouse,

55

scrambling after my older brother and sister. They were both tall and long of stride, wearing functional bows and arrows slung over their warrior-like shoulders, while I trotted behind like their pet dog. I didn't mind. I was only ten years old and Simon and Julia were my heroes. They took me on forbidden adventures in the forest. Our parents didn't allow us outside the farm property because of the threat of stray revolutionaries, but Simon and Julia flagrantly disobeyed them. It probably started on a dare that escalated out of hand. It was as much that dare as anything else that ended up saving one life, sacrificing another and damning the third.

We often spent the better part of the day in the forest and fields beyond the farm property. It was only Simon, who usually made the decision in the first place to stay all day, who had the presence of mind to bring along food—which he seldom shared. During our journey Simon would usually throw a glance back once or twice to make sure I was still keeping up and rebuke my snail's pace: "Hey dreamer, hurry up or we'll leave you behind!" Julia would snap at him in my defense: "Claire's only ten, you idiot! So slow down for the runt!" They would always argue. "Well, you slow down too, then!" he'd shout back. "I slowed down for you already, slug!" she'd rejoin. On it would go as they shoved each other until I caught up to them. They were less than a year apart and I think Julia resented Simon being the eldest and the one who made all the decisions. She wanted to make them but she never did, so she always disagreed with his.

The day started pretty much like any other day. Simon and Julia were arguing as usual by the time we reached the forest. They'd overheard a discussion between Mom and Tante Lise about the revolution.

We moved to the country last summer to get away from the fighting in Montreal. Mom and Dad lost their jobs because of the Gaian revolution. The company they worked for, BioGen Technologies, went up in smoke thanks to the latest rash of fire bombings and Mom got scared that the Gaians would come after the survivors; mainly Dad, who was one of the head honchos there. So we packed up and moved to my Oncle Pierre's and Tante Lise's small dairy farm in the Eastern Townships, where the air smelled clean…well, cleaner than the cities, anyway.

Mom and Dad met at BioGen in Montreal. She was a junior microbiologist in "functional genomics" with unorthodox ideas, and he was one of their chief scientists in nano-technology and transgenic research. BioGen was supposed to save the world, but then one of Dad's "creations" got away from them and crashed the world's wheat crop.

"Tante Lise shouldn't call Dad Frankenstein," Julia grumbled. "He isn't a monster."

"It's 'cause he *made* monsters, stupid." Simon snorted. "Frankenstein's the name of the mad scientist, not the clone monsters he made."

"He's not a mad scientist," she defended. "And they're not monsters!"

"The Gaians say they are," Simon quipped, picking his teeth. "They say that BioGen's just another multi-national company that's making too much money. They say BioGen's technology is irresponsible and that stuff Dad did is wrecking our ecosystems like diversity, evolution and stuff."

"What do the Gaians know. They're luddites," Julia said with disgust, parroting what our father always said. I knew she didn't know what a luddite was. "Dad just made a little mistake once. Some DNA escaped and went rogue on them. Part of the risk we have to take in GE crops."

"Yeah, like widespread famine," Simon muttered, shaking his head.

Julia frowned with worry. "Tante Lise isn't a Gaian…is she?"

"Dunno." Simon shrugged and absently raked back his mat of straw-coloured hair with his hands. "She doesn't like what Dad was doing. Lots of people think it's wrong. Even Mom."

"Mom's just scared they'll find us," Julia grumbled. "She's scared of everything," she murmured more to herself than to Simon, as if trying to convince herself.

As we stepped out of the cool dappled forest into the warm sunshine of a small clearing, Simon announced that we should eat some lunch. I was happy to comply.

"It's only ten-thirty," Julia objected.

"Well, I'm hungry. So it's time to eat."

"You can't tell *me* when to eat," Julia said tartly. "Pig!"

"That's because you only brought along some crackers while I made three sandwiches for me! You're never prepared," he said smugly. "And now you're jealous!"

"I'm not jealous," Julia said haughtily. "I'm just not hungry."

"You are."

"Am not!" Her face went pink.

"Are too, dork!" He laughed, then promptly sat down on a patch of matted long grass and swung out his backpack. Without waiting for either of us to agree or join him, Simon fished out a peanut butter and raspberry jam sandwich and bolted it down with gluttonous pleasure as I longed in silence. He wasn't a particularly tidy eater and left a smear of red jam on his chin. I noticed that his cheeks were flushed already from the heat and sweat glistened on his nose and forehead.

Julia stomped around then finally dropped down and threw her arms against her upraised knees. She glowered at her older brother. Even if she *was* hungry she wasn't going to admit to it now. I was ready to confess my hunger in hopes of receiving a morsel, but Julie glared at me as if she'd read my mind. My shoulders drooped in defeat.

After Simon finished his first course of lunch, we plunged back into the forest out of the burning sun. The deer flies buzzed furiously around our heads amid wild arm waving and frustrated outcries. Simon led us up a hill toward a large hemlock grove. He scrambled a steep incline to a narrow long ledge that may have once been a path. The forest floor was carpeted with dead needles and tiny fallen cones and dotted with young maple saplings. Like a man who had found gold, Simon bent down and gathered a handful of cones then darted behind a tree. Julia waited for me catch up before she scrambled up, shrieking at the deluge of cones Simon flung at her face. He sniggered as she practically fell backwards on top of me. She swore furiously at him, her face red with embarrassment.

"Come on!" Simon said enthusiastically. "Let's play war!"

Eager to play, Julia ran for cover and gathered her own arsenal of weapons.

"You can't use your hands!" Simon warned just as Julia was about to throw some cones at him. "You have to make a slingshot using a tree like this." He squatted over a young sapling and bent its branches into a mutilated mess, fit a cone into his makeshift catapult, pulled the sapling back than let it spring naturally towards Julia. The cone flew past her head, barely missing her. Both participants shrieked with pleasure.

As Julia and Simon collected their cones, I, left out of the game as usual, sat back like a dutiful and appreciative audience to watch their creative entertainment. The warriors shot in earnest, sometimes hitting their opponent with a victorious cry, other times, most of the time, missing widely. In the process the poor saplings they used were swiftly demolished and they had to forage for a new catapult. During one of her forages, Julia tripped on an exposed root and fell headlong to the ground with a hollow thud. When she didn't get up right away, Simon jeered, "Hey, clone monster! Get up!"

She jerked to her feet. She wiped her head and pushed

back her thick mane of chestnut hair, tucking it behind her ears. I noticed a cut on her dirt-smeared forehead. "Don't call me that, you moron!" she said, temper flaring.

"*You're* the moron! You never do anything on your own," he bit out. "That's 'cause Dad made you out of spare parts back at the lab!" That line was usually reserved for me and I was used to it. But Julia couldn't bear the insult.

"You shut up!" she screamed. "I'm tired of your snotty remarks about Dad. You can keep them to yourself—"

"Until he gets us all killed when they come looking for 'Doctor Frankenstein'!" Simon mocked.

Julia bolted at him, hands lashing out like raptor's talons. He jerked out of her clawing hands and tackled her. They rolled among the dead leaves, hands swiping and legs kicking. I couldn't tell who was winning, but both were crying.

"Stop it! Stop it!" I pleaded and tried to pry them apart. I finally succeeded but only after receiving a kick in the stomach.

Simon stood up first, nose bleeding and an eye already swollen. "You bitch!" he screamed down at her as she pushed herself off the ground and wiped her dirty tear-stained face. "You crazy bitch! You don't care about Mom. You're just like Dad: he should have thought about us before he went and made all those monsters!"

"Go to hell!" she shrieked. "You don't have a clue what he was doing. He was feeding the hungry of the world!"

"Yeah? Meantime we're polluting it so much we're killing everyone we're feeding!"

"Can't we do both?" I piped up. "Like the plants?"

"What?" They both turned haltingly to me like I was an alien who'd just uttered gibberish.

"Feed the hungry *and* clean up the pollution," I said. One day while my brother and sister were in school, my father had pulled me out of class to take me on a tour of the BioGen facility and show me their artificial photosynthesis lab: "How marvelous," he'd exulted, "if we could copy what chloroplasts do and plug directly into the sun without burning a drop of oil. No more hungry people. No more fossil fuel and no more pollution."

He'd dropped me off at my mother's lab and she'd shown me holo-images generated through electron tomography of mitochondria and chloroplasts. While my father had dedicated himself to feeding the starving masses, my mother dreamed of a world where people no longer needed to eat. The mitochondria and chloroplasts shared a common ancestry, she explained to me. They both descended from earlier prokaryotic cells that established themselves as internal symbionts, endosymbionts, we now call them, of a larger anaerobic cell. The similarities between these two organelles were uncanny, my mother went on: for instance, they both contained their own DNA and ribosomes; they divided by themselves and used the same enzyme to produce energy in the form of ATP. The only major difference was how they produced ATP. While chloroplasts used chlorophyll to capture the sun's energy, mitochondria broke down glucose in the food we eat. Inspired by my father's tools and my mother's vision, I soared on a dream of people capable of photosynthesis in a Ciamician world.

"Mom told me," my words rushed out in a torrent. I knew I had seconds before they ignored me again. "She told me about a scientist named Giacomo Ciamician who a hundred years ago dreamed of a world where photosynthesis did everything for us—"

Julia took in a sharp breath and turned back to rail at Simon: "You're so narrow-minded, just like a Gaian, just like Mom!" She retrieved her bow, scattered arrows and quiver. "Come on, Claire." Julia took my hand with a last glare at Simon, who was brushing off the mess from his shirt and pants. "We're going home." Without waiting for me to decide, she led me at a brisk pace back to the farm.

"Do that!" Simon yelled after us, and sat down on a rock to sulk. I turned my head for a last glimpse of him as Julia tugged me hard down the hill.

"Shouldn't we wait for him?" I asked innocently when I lost sight of him.

"He can find his own way home," she muttered, tugging me harder. "He led us here, didn't he?"

I staggered over the rough terrain to keep up, secretly praying that Julia knew the way. It wasn't Simon I was worried about. The sun disappeared behind carbon-coloured clouds. They scudded overhead like prey, chased by a biting wind. It howled and sent the Trembling Aspens thrashing above us. Their lanky poles clanked like bones to the moaning wind as the leaves hissed a mad chorus.

"What if we meet a bear?" I asked, starting to feel unsafe.

"There aren't any bears in the forest, Claire," Julia said shaking her head sarcastically at me. "Besides, I have my bow and arrows." She tapped her quiver and bow smugly. She was right, I thought, pacified by her confidence. She was good with that thing and I was a little surprised that she didn't remind me of the four rabbits and two coyotes she'd killed while all Simon had managed to do with his was wound a single rabbit.

We broke through the perimeter of the dense forest that lined the farm as rain pelted us like missiles, instantly drenching us. As if the stinging rain had warned her, Julia gripped my arm to stay me. I saw her eyes harden as she threw swift glances to the open garden gate and the greenhouse whose door was ajar—

I squeaked in surprise as she clamped a hand over my mouth. "Shhh! Hold still!" she whispered, glaring at me under streams of wet hair. Then she let go and I couldn't stop trembling while she snatched her bow and loaded it with an arrow. As if in response to her move, the front door of the farmhouse creaked open and a large unshaven man with unwashed hair and eyes glinting of malice lumbered out. He carried a loaded sack in one dirty hand and a blood-covered knife in the other. The man spotted us and I hitched my breath, stiff with terror, not daring to blink the rain off my eyelashes. He grinned, baring yellow teeth, and stomped toward us. I scrambled behind Julia and clutched the leg of her shorts.

Julia glanced from the man's churlish grin to his knife and raised her bow. He laughed at her. Without hesitation she drew the bow back and let the arrow fly. It sunk into his chest and he inhaled sharply, eyes bulging in disbelief. Then he charged us. I cringed and wet my pants. Julia stood like a statue, her arm a blur of reloading, and struck him with two or more arrows before he staggered and fell dead on his face only meters from us.

Gruff laughter from the side of the house warned us that there were more men. Julia seized my arm and dove for cover in a small thicket by the cherry tree just as Simon broke through the forest into the clearing. I shivered, cowering in our wet hiding place as several armed men marched past us toward the dead man. Toward Simon. He stood not far from their dead colleague, hair hanging in his eyes and bow in his hand. They made the logical conclusion.

He must have made his own rightful conclusion and his eyes fleetingly strayed, searching hard, beyond the thugs to where we huddled behind them. Did he see us there? I imagined that he did. But before I could see more, Julia shoved my face down into the dirt. What I didn't see I could only imagine as my heart slammed up my throat: Simon's and Julia's eyes locking, their anguished message of agreement. The rest I heard through the hissing rain: a slashing sound, a clipped gasp and a thud. I was choking but didn't dare struggle. Hot tears stung my eyes. Julia's firm hand, now shaking, kept me down for an eternity of smelling dirt and rotting vegetation. Of feeling the wet prickle of soil and leaves against my face. Of listening to men's grunts and shuffling steps dwindle to a constant sizzle and plopping of rain.

I was young, but I knew perfectly well what had just happened: Simon took the hit for us, and Julia let him. The first—and last—decision they'd made together was one made in complicity.

α

Julia and I made it out of there, after she confirmed that Simon was dead and found our parents and relatives murdered inside the house. We had a difficult journey but were eventually taken in by a kind family, where we rode out the remaining years of war until the Gaians established a new government and peace was reinstated.

I found a calling in micro-biomimicry—the Gaian's answer to aimless technology—at Concordia University in Montreal. Julia never returned to school. She got a job as a waitress and helped me through university. I met André, a med student, and eventually married while Julia wandered like a nomad from one relationship to another. We saw less and less of one another, until I started to think she was avoiding me. When she committed suicide I was shocked. But not surprised.

Had she been running the same thought loop I had? How it might have played if she hadn't killed that Gaian and run instead.

Had she needlessly killed a man—albeit a murderer—and needlessly caused Simon's death? If we'd run instead, would they have chased us or let us go? They were paid assassins, after all, on a mission to 'take out' our father. Not child murderers. Maybe Simon would still be with us and Julia wouldn't have destroyed herself out of irreconcilable guilt for her inaction in Simon's murder—on account of her initial violence—to save the two of us....

Or had she tapped into some divine providence when she let the arrow fly and saved my life the only way it could have been saved...at Simon's expense...and consequently her own?...

α

I turn to the audience and spot André and our two children. They blur through my tears. As a scientist I understand that one cannot know the future or one's destiny; but my heart tells me differently. Like most things for him, my brother's choice was clearly laid before him. For Julia, as always, it was not so simple. And yet, that spring day she became more than she was and with fluid motions enacted her part in the cruel miracle that brought me here today.

The heaviness in my legs lifts as I take the last steps to the podium in the open-air auditorium that celebrates our clean air. I am finally ready to accept my Nobel Prize. And I know at last what I am going to say:

I'm here today accepting this award for the creation of photosynthetic symbionts in human mitochondria, because of my brother and sister. I share this honor with them. If not for their heroism on a day long ago, I would not have survived with the burning motivation and tenacity to pursue a lifelong dream: to serve the human race and the planet with the gift of an alternate and clean source of fuel and food—a way for humanity to directly harness energy from the sun...

Julia's gift.

The Mark of a Genius

"I'm Jorge," he extended his hand.

Mitch accepted his firm handshake as excitement surged up her cheeks She'd noticed his dignified face earlier in the crowded room of strangers and his gaze had briefly met hers then strayed away, somehow disappointing her. She was used to men looking at her. Since the age of seventeen boys had undressed her with their eyes. But this man's glancing stare betrayed a kind of recognition that sent her heart pumping in her throat with a fearful thrill: *could he be one too?*

[SAM], she'd sent her thought wave to her AI-partner. [Find out everything you can on the person I'm watching].

[OKAY, MITCH], SAM had replied in her head.

Mitch had caught furtive glimpses of the stranger as he wandered among the other guests then lost sight of him. She'd boldly searched the room, unconsciously straightening her dress only to flinch when she found him standing right in front of her with an enigmatic smile.

"You're Mitch, aren't you?" he said in a pleasant tenor's voice, his handsome lean face radiating a disquieting calm.

"Michelin," she corrected rather tartly, fighting down her rising defensiveness; no one called her Mitch except her best friend.

"Your boss pointed you out to me earlier," he explained, drawing her to a more secluded corner of the room. "First time to one of these, Michelin?" He waved his hand toward the crowd.

66

"Yes," she said, irked at herself for blushing. Was it so obvious? Kraken had insisted that she accompany him to this fancy outer-city party. She'd come just to please her new boss and worn the only good dress she owned.

Jorge tipped his head sideways and a network of lines radiated from his sudden blue eyes. "Kraken calls you a genius, but I know you're a veemeld."

Her heart slammed and she bristled, eyes involuntarily darting around to make sure no one had overheard his accusation. Now she knew why she'd been repelled and attracted to him at the same time. She'd guessed right earlier: he was a veemeld too. A rude one.

"I'm sorry," he said softly, offering a conciliatory smile. "I didn't mean to insult you. I'm also a veemeld. You hide it well. I didn't sense you."

And why should he? she thought peevishly. She tended to block her thoughts from other veemelds. And Jorge wasn't being too intrusive — not like that scruffy vagrant boy, Dexter, she'd run into earlier today near her shack in the inner-city. The little brat had followed her home again and when she'd turned to glare at him his thoughts burst into hers like the groping hands of an inexperienced lover. He'd plowed right into her mind, blundered into the front door of her brain in the excitement of sensing another veemeld's energy field. Jorge had only flirted in a back alley of her mind, gently probing via their respective AI-partners. He'd guessed the rest.

"Your avatar is?..." Jorge trailed, obviously hoping she'd provide the answer.

Mitch gave him a crooked smile and obliged, "SAM. My AI-entity's called SAM."

Jorge's eyes sparkled. "Ah." He looked impressed. "Short for Samantha?"

"Smart Analog Machine."

"Ah." He nodded. "SAM has quite a reputation in the core. I should have known it was 'you'."

There followed a moment of silence. Then Jorge leaned closer, his eyes penetrating, and confided, "It's lonely being a veemeld, isn't it."

Her face flared. Unable to meet his probing eyes, Michelin dropped her gaze. She found herself staring down her cleavage past her black silk dress to her long bare legs and thinking that her dress was too tight and too short. Was he coming on to her?

"They treat us more like tools than people," Jorge went on in her silence. Michelin looked up into his sad eyes. "When I announced that I was a veemeld in school, the other students harassed me. My bosses use me like a commodity to be traded or disposed of." He exhaled slowly and ran his long fingers through his gray hair. "When researchers developed the AI-core and the technology to use it, they had no idea that only five percent of the population could veemeld with it."

"Actually, it's *two* percent."

He smiled wryly. "In any case, it's rather sad," he continued with a thoughtful expression. "Since scientists have now proven that just through the act of veemelding, we improve our cognition, memory and learning, particularly our ability to respond to changing environmental information. We do it through activation—"

"Of theta rhythm in the hippocampus. Yes, I know. We use the high-frequency tetanic pulses generated by the AI-core to activate a particular phase of theta rhythm during veemeld."

Jorge nodded enthusiastically. "Every part of the brain that's enhanced in veemelds is involved in theta rhythm: the brain stem that transmits signals to the septum, which then activates T.R. in the hippocampus and the entorhinal cortex. While in normal people it's REM sleep that activates theta rhythm, veemelds have it on all the time. Remarkable, isn't it?"

He slipped his elegant hands into his pockets. "Your whole body is a symphony of rhythms, a vehicle of spontaneous, persistent synchrony. Fireflies talk with light; planets speak through the force of gravity; heart cells share electric currents. We...." His eyes fired with emotion. "Imagine what humanity could be if we all connected like a single autopoietic system in a kind of synchronal dance."

Mitch shrugged. She didn't usually have time for dreamers...and Jorge was obviously a dreamer. She indulged him anyway: "Autopoietic?"

Jorge smiled like he'd won a prize: her attentive ear, she supposed. "I'm talking about the whole of our society behaving and evolving in a self-organized, adaptive way. We already do this—veemelds, that is. Have been long before the AI-technology came along."

She gave him a skeptical half-smile. "People 'veemelding' without the AI-core?"

"Proof is all around us, Michelin, in the independent formulation of calculus by Newton and Leibniz, or the theory of the evolution of species by Charles Darwin and Alfred Russel Wallace. Then there's McFadden and Pocket independently but simultaneously theorizing that electromagnetic fields are the seat of our consciousness. Multiple independent discoveries have increased in society a thousand-fold since the nineteenth century. Did you know that? The reason is obvious: the fabric of our society is evolving into a neural network, learning, interacting and sharing—moving toward the achievement of a common zeitgeist."

Mitch folded her arms across her chest. "That doesn't prove the existence of veemelds then."

Jorge's eyes lit to her challenge. "Well, there are two schools of thought on multiple independent discoveries: that it's a function of either social context or the qualities of the individuals making the discovery such as inventive genius. I think it's both. I think most of our geniuses were frustrated veemelds waiting for a better vehicle to tap into—the quantum electromagnetic waves of the AI-core—but they made do with humanity's subtle autopoietic system instead."

Mitch caught herself smirking. Jorge hadn't struck her as arrogant; yet he was suggesting that every genius from Newton to Einstein was a veemeld! But she couldn't help thinking his premise elegant. Scientists had figured out that the unique genetic makeup of veemelds provided them with, among other things, a slightly different electromagnetic field arrangement, one better suited to sending and receiving non-local fields outside their bodies. Which explained why veemelds, alone, could...well, veemeld.

As though he was reading her thoughts, Jorge went on, "When McFadden and Pocket simultaneously but independently proposed the theory of a localized electromagnetic field as the seat of consciousness a hundred years ago, they had no idea what a Pandora's Box they'd opened. We now know that there are many different kinds of energy fields with differing frequencies and waveforms surrounding our brains and our entire bodies and connecting us to the rest of the planet and universe, like—"

"Static and pulsed EM, quantum-vacuum fields, gravitational fields and cosmic and particle-mediated fields to name a few," Mitch leapt in, not to be outdone. She was Kraken's "genius" after all.

Jorgen nodded with a thoughtful smile. "I thought that perhaps all humans—veemelds and non-veemelds—could eventually communicate as we are meant to—as a single autopoietic system, through the subtle force fields that embrace all life and non-living entities of our planet and universe. Imagine a world where there's no war because we all communicate and understand one another."

How naïve he was! "You're suggesting that geniuses— veemelds—" She fought down a sneer "—are simply more in tune with cosmic forces, so they can tap into?..." She trailed with a shrug.

"The web of our greater consciousness," he finished for her, quite serious. "The autopoietic network of our humanity... waves of consciousness."

"Waves of consciousness," she repeated, finding it hard to hide the jeering tone that crept into her voice. "A new kind of energy field? Surfing the consciousness wave?" She felt a sarcastic smile tugging at her lips.

"Far-fetched, you think?" His eyes gripped hers. "It's not so different from what we already know is true. EM-mediated consciousness, for instance, and non-localized wave propagation. Researchers have long known about the phenomenon of 'collective effect,' Michelin. The synchronicity of multicellular organisms and societies of insects are good examples of 'collective consciousness,' and 'social facilitation.' Either way, we're the key. Veemelds. We're the nodes of the human network. I'm convinced that all humans are capable of it. They just need to be taught. By us." He smiled wistfully. Then he exhaled and the fire in his eyes died. "Just a dream, I suppose." Jorge stroked his jaw pensively. "If anything we're growing more isolated and distrustful."

His words resonated in her gut and she dropped her gaze to the floor again. It was a wonderful dream nevertheless.

Jorge pursed his lips, letting his gaze stray for a moment to a distant place. When he refocused on her, his eyes glinted and his voice took on an edge. "They fear us, Michelin—what we can do: talk to machines in our heads. Run the city. The luddites among us have turned that fear to hatred. They're terrified by our unique connection with the AI-community. We're dangerous freaks to them. Genetic monsters. Cyborgs...."

Machine-sluts....

"We have no mark to show what we are," Jorge went on, "so we can choose to hide in our anonymity. The luddites would like to change that. Brand us with some visible mark. That's one of the reasons I formed the Veemeld Alliance. Do you know about us?"

"Yes," she said guardedly.

"But you haven't joined us." Jorge looked puzzled. He pulled out a durable card and pressed it warmly in her hand. "We're having a meeting tonight, in fact. At my place." Then his eyes glowed like a warm camp fire. "I'd like to be a friend." His sincere expression drew her in. "A *real* friend."

Longing swelled up her throat and made her swallow convulsively. She knew what he meant: a friend who knew what she was.

He tilted his head and gazed at her with intense curiosity. "You don't have any friends, Michelin. Yet you've lived here for a year, the longest time you've stayed in one place."

Mitch jerked her hand out of his and clenched her jaw. That wasn't true, she fumed. She had Nancy, after all. Her best friend….She thought again….Nancy didn't know she was a veemeld. If she did, would they still be friends? Mitch had long ago learned to move, rather than face the consequences of intimacy. Her gaze darted around the room, looking for Kraken.

Jorge continued in a soft voice, "Veemelds can be fiercely independent and secretive. Whenever we conceal something of ourselves we choose to become slaves to our secret."

She knew he meant her.

"It's only together in open solidarity that we can overcome the prejudice—the fear and hatred—against us. Perhaps we can teach them that they don't need to fear us." His eyes grew intense and she fought the urge to back away. "Michelin, we need you." He drew closer to her and she recoiled. "Our community needs you. You're intelligent and….

very attractive. You'd make an excellent spokesperson for us. With your help we could take charge of our destiny and move the human race forward to embrace a harmony of diversity. Everyone needs a friend, Michelin. Including you."

Mitch felt anger heat her face. She didn't need his solidarity or his friendship. She'd done just fine on her own up to now. She gave Jorge back his card. "I'm sorry but I'm not interested in joining your alliance. I'm happy just being an Icarian."

He blinked several times then stuttered, his voice rising a pitch, "But, how can you say that? You can never be just an Icarian—"

"Because I'm a...*genius*?" she scoffed and brushed past him. "Good day."

She glimpsed his crestfallen face as she walked briskly to the other side of the room where Kraken stood, talking to another man. Kraken leered down at her and enveloped her in his arm like a possession. She felt a hollow in the pit of her stomach.

Mitch excused herself early from the party and took the tube-jet home. She watched the amber emergency lights strobe past her as the tube-jet dove into the darkness of the tunnel. She saw Jorge's kind face in her mind and found herself thinking about that miserable day when the girls at school discovered what she was....

φ

Eager to make a good impression on her new school friend, Mitch was helping Abbie, who was struggling with her Ecology 101 lesson. They were sharing a holo-module at the Ed-Center when Abbie turned from the holo-com to Mitch, seated beside her. "Here's my answer to his question on the principals of Icarian ecology," she confided. "'Ecosystems develop through natural selection from generally chaotic, pioneer stages toward stable ordered stages which maintain a dynamic equilibrium through internal forces.'"

"No, Abbie, that thinking's a hundred years out of date. Ecosystems function and change under *stable chaos*, naturally cycling through destructive and building phases through changing variables—"

"Nonsense!" a gruff voice scolded. Michelin flinched and looked up at the teacher who towered over her. She fought not to cower under his glare. "You're quoting heretical theories, young woman!"

She focused on his dark nostrils and said in a shaky voice, "But I read—"

"*Read!*" he cut her off. Several other students peered round their cubicles. "More like *cheated* by slutting with your AI friends for information." The teacher leaned over her and his small eyes narrowed. "I won't have you disrupting my class." He sneered to her look of horror. He'd just given her away. "Yes, *I know what you are,*" he ended menacingly. He stalked away as gawking faces ducked behind the cubicles.

During break Mitch was looking for Abbie in the school mall when a classmate collided with her. "Out of my way, *veemeld!*" the girl snarled.

Mitch backed away. "I'm not a veemeld," she lied.

"Yes you are." The girl sneered. "I heard the teacher." Several other girls closed in on her, forming a ring.

"Veemeld! Veemeld!" they chanted, shoving her until she fell to the ground. "AI slut—"

Mitch scrambled up in angry defense. "I'm not a vee—"

A fist struck her on the mouth, splitting her lip. "Veemeld slut!"

Her lip pounded and she tasted blood. The girls pressed against her, their faces distorted with hatred. They pummeled her as the chant resumed. "Veemeld! Veemeld!" Voices built, echoing like a mantra, to the increasing rhythm of their blows. Mitch tucked her head down and raised both arms to protect her face and chest, taking the blows with her shoulders and back.

"Hey!" A teacher approached. The girls scattered like flies disturbed from a carcass. Mitch fled in the opposite direction, glancing back. "Yes, you! Stop!" The teacher shouted at her. She rushed into the closest bathroom and, finding an empty cubicle, slid in and slammed the door shut. She slumped on the toilet, elbows on her knees, and cradled her head in her hands, rocking and sobbing, and hearing the hum of those cursed AI machines in her head.

She was getting so tired of moving....

Mitch was the only one who got out at the inner-city station. She inhaled the familiar stink of urine, stale liquor and rotting garbage as she picked her way past shiny pools of spit and pies of dried vomit to the stairway that led outside. Mitch bolted the stairs two by two to the exit and flung open the door. She took in a deep inhale of fresh air and shivered in the bracing cool air. Wrapping her bare arms around her waist for warmth, she headed home at a brisk pace and watched the long jerking shadow of herself that the pale moon threw ahead of her. She found herself stealing glances at the dozens of bivouacs that littered the street: eclectic shacks, built from the scrap of discarded droids, abandoned furniture, even parts of an old tube-jet, and cemented with the detritus of urban fast-living. Her shack wasn't much better but it was home...for now. This was the roughest part of town. Hell, she'd lived in worse places. One just had to be smart and careful—

She'd just turned a corner to the shortcut she normally took when her stomach clenched at the sound of grunts, shouting and malicious laughter that drifted up the dark alley. Heart pulsing in her throat, Mitch stole forward. When she emerged from the alley into a courtyard, she saw five teenage boys beating a younger boy—*Oh, no*...unmistakable, the chaotic hair and the rags he wore: it was Dexter, the young veemeld who kept following her home.

He must have caught her emotional surge because his head jerked round and he looked right at her even though she was still hidden in the shadows of the alley. [Please! Help me!] came his outburst.

Mitch threw her gaze around in search of another bystander. No luck. The place was empty save the boy's attackers and her. Mitch gripped her lower lip in her teeth, feeling a surge of adrenalin. Dexter was too young and feral to command respect from the AI-community, but she was another matter. She squared her shoulders then stepped out into the light and shouted in a commanding voice, "Stop that now!"

The boys halted and stared at her. She caught several lecherous grins and pulled down on her short dress. Dexter whimpered on the ground and the leader, a square-faced boy with spiked hair pointed down at him. "He's a freaking veemeld!" he said as though it fully explained their actions. "Stay out of it, lady."

"I mean it," she said and marched toward them, hands balled at her sides. "Stop right now! You're hurting him!"

"What's it to you?" The leader spat out. It suddenly dawned on him: "You're one too, aren't you? A fucking freak."

"No way, Russ," one of the other boys interjected, licking his lips. "She's too luscious to be a veemeld." Several of the other boys agreed.

I could slink out of there, Mitch thought. Just like all the times before. They didn't want to believe she was a veemeld; she could take advantage of her beauty and retreat back into the shadows. They probably wouldn't kill Dexter. She could let him fend for himself, like she'd fended for herself all these years....

Then her eyes flickered over Dexter's cowering form, head tucked in and both arms raised to protect his face and chest. She fired back, "Yes!" she practically gasped the word and felt the terrifying exhilaration of unburdening herself. "I am." The words surged up her throat like an electric charge, burning all the way up: "I'm a veemeld too!"

A few boys moaned in disappointment, scanning her covetously. "What a waste of good babe meat," one of them sighed.

The leader sneered as she resumed her advance. "Once we're finished here, you'll have your turn," he said. The other boys followed with enthusiastic noises. "Grab the AI-slut!" he commanded, pointing to her. Two boys dashed for her with churlish grins.

Mitch fought from recoiling. "I'm sorry, but you won't be doing that either," she said. The two boys sniggered.

Mitch clenched her teeth but stood her ground.

[SAM], she sent her thought wave to her AI-companion. [Instruct the security system of Liv-Building E-29 to dispose of the five boys engaged in criminal activities, beta 050 and 051. Visual through my retina].

[OKAY, MITCH], SAM responded inside her head. Instantly, several ports on the building swiveled and discharged a concussion laser beam at the five boys, stunning them. They crumpled to the ground in unison, like a strangely choreographed macabre ballet. The two who'd rushed her tumbled a meter from her. Mitch side-stepped them and rushed to Dexter, who lay curled up in a fetal position, entwined with limp arms and legs. As she bent over him, Mitch continued her thought to SAM: [instruct security droids of Region E to collect these five hoodlums and put them into the cooler. They can use my visual for the crime record].

[OKAY, MITCH. THEY'RE ON THEIR WAY].

[Thanks, SAM]. Mitch touched Dexter and he flinched. "It's okay," she said in a gentle voice. "You're safe now."

Dexter looked up, wide-eyed, through a dirt-smeared face and cracked a big grin, revealing a bloody mouth, which didn't seem to concern him anymore. "You did it, didn't you? You got the AIs to blast 'em! I knew you were a veemeld. That was awesome...."

She realized that she didn't need to answer his steady stream of questions and exclamations. "Can you get up?" She helped him to his feet. "I'll take you to my place and clean you up. Looks like you've got a few nasty cuts."

They left the courtyard for her shack as the city's security droids arrived. When they arrived at her place, Mitch pulled out her first aid kit, sat Dexter down by the sink in the bathroom and gently washed his mouth before applying some antiseptic healing gel.

"Looks like they were trying to shut you up," she observed with a wry smile, thinking of how he'd poked his mind where he had no business being.

"Yeah," Dexter said. "I keep telling everyone I'm a veemeld."

Mitch snorted. "Why on Earth would you do that?" She snapped the first aid kit shut and leaned against the sink to give him a long hard look. "You don't look dumb."

"How else will I find someone who'll like me for what I am?" he answered simply.

"And you're willing to get beat up time and time again to find that person?"

He nodded and gave her a goofy smile despite his puffy split lip. "I found you."

Mitch felt a strange mixture of emotions swell into her throat. "Come on," she finally said. "I know someone who wants to meet you, then. A whole community."

φ

When Jorge opened the door he gasped. "What a surprise!" He beamed with undisguised pleasure, glancing from Mitch to Dexter. "Come in, come in!" He swung the door open for them to enter. A dozen or so people engaged in desultory conversation were already seated in comfortable chairs in Jorge's living room. The meeting must have started already, Mitch observed.

She waved her hand at the boy. "This is Dexter. He's a veemeld too. Like us," she ended with a half-smile. "I told him he'd find a few genuine friends here."

Jorge nodded with enthusiastic approval. "I'm sure he will. Hello, Dexter."

Jorge was about to introduce both of them to the other veemelds in the room, when Mitch touched his arm. "And," she added in a lowered voice, "I've reconsidered what you asked. I'd like to try being a spokesperson for veemelds...."

She noticed that the room was suddenly quiet and everyone was looking at her.

"Thank you, Michelin," Jorge said, taking her hand and pressing it between his two.

She pressed back. "You can all me Mitch," she said, her smile opening to a broad grin.

Neither Here Nor There

She's wandered the purple landscape for days...she thinks. She can't be sure because the sun never rises or sets and she never gets hungry or thirsty. She's seen no sign of inhabitants, no roads, fences or buildings in the distant rolling hills. Not even wildlife. No twittering bird or sound of a scampering rodent. The silence is unbearable. There isn't even a breeze to stir her hair or brace her cheeks. Nothing. She drops her gaze to the ground, which resembles a pointillist water colour of a field with flowers and grass.

Maybe she's caved in on herself and is seeing the universe through a fractal lens, visualizing the Planck nodes of spin networks: space and time made of discrete pieces.

She feels like she's in limbo and supposes that she is. That's what this place is, after all, she reasons. An in-between place for those like her. She bites down on her lip and draws in a long breath. Did she make a mistake in her choice?...No, she concludes. No mistake. She deserves this. Besides, the alternatives are unimaginable, she thinks, recalling the horrible scene....

π

"Have a seat, Miss Cross," a pleasant male voice coming from behind startled her and spun her around. She stood beside a long table in a spacious but ornate room that smelled of oak and lemon. She had no idea how she'd gotten here or who the fair-haired, clean-cut gentleman standing in front of her was. She'd thought that she was alone in the room. Tilting her head slightly, she studied his pleasant features: tangles of curly blond hair fell to his shoulders as he eyed her with kind eyes and an honest mouth. He stood dignified in a white smock, coattails and breeches, white leather boots and gold jewellery. Impeccably groomed, he looked rather like a dandy or perhaps a regal version of Mr. Clean. "How about there," he pointed with a kind smile to one of the ornate oak chairs to her right. "That'll do, don't you think, Luce?"

"I told you not to call me that," a basso voice growled behind her and she spun around again to see a rakishly handsome, dark-haired man slouched, brooding, in a chair at one end of the table. This was spooky; he hadn't been there a moment ago. His scruffy face sported a goatee and his eyes flashed with mischief. He looked unkempt in a black leather jacket over a grey t-shirt and tight jeans. He crossed a leg over his thigh and ran his long fingers through his hair, smirking at her. "Sit, sit, Lara," he said, flicking his hand to the chair impatiently, and flashed her a predatory grin. As if answering her silent question, he added, "You'll find out soon enough."

Lara dropped into the indicated chair and sat stiff with worry. Not that the sight of these two incredibly handsome men, both of whom seemed to covet her with their eyes, wasn't entirely unpleasant. It was just that she couldn't remember how she got here, or, in fact, where she'd been just prior....

The two men exchanged a knowing look and in a sudden plummeting moment she recalled the disastrous scene that had brought her here. She gasped and slipped from her seat, clamping her eyes shut against the horrible vision of shooting her brother and then herself. Lara found it too much to bear.

"No!" she cried out in despair, rising to her knees and grabbing her head. "This must be a nightmare! I-d-didn't kill him—did I? Oh, God!"

"Yes?" The blonde man was instantly at her side. He pressed her head to his shoulder and stroked her hair. "It's all right, Lara. Let it out. Let the healing begin." She found his soft voice very comforting and let the tears flow.

"Oh, cut the crap, Yah," the dark-haired man snarled. "It's not all right. She's dead. And she *did* do it. You always take advantage of them when they first come here."

Lara blinked and rose to her feet with the other man's help. Slow understanding gripped her as the fair-haired man took the seat opposite the dark-haired man. She sat back in her chair, between them, and gazed from one end of the long table to the other. "You're not—I mean, you and you," she looked from one to the other: Mr. Clean and Mr. Dirt. They both gave her an awkward, almost embarrassed smile. As though they'd been caught doing something they weren't supposed to do. "But you don't look like—"

"Satan and God?"

"God and Satan?" they said together.

"This is how you pictured us, though," God offered, looking embarrassed again. Satan shrugged and gazed at the ceiling.

Lara contemplated the consequences with a thoughtful frown. "That means I'm either in Hell or in Heaven—"

"Not so fast, chicky-pop." Satan waved his hand at her. "This is where we all decide where you go." He turned brusquely to God with a determined look. "And I say she comes with me."

"What? You're kidding!" said God and Lara at the same time.

"She killed a man, Yah," Satan insisted. "She's mine."

"I told you not to call me that!" God said, suddenly looking undignified as he stood up and pouted. "It was an act of altruism," he went on, leaning forward and resting both hands on the table. His eyes grew intense and they flashed like lightening. "She saved him from his own torment and from raping more women. The man heard voices telling him to hurt people—probably *your* voice."

"Don't blame me, Yah," Satan scoffed, swinging his long legs onto the polished table, black leather cowboy boots hammering the surface with a loud bang. "You gave him schizophrenia in the first place. And we all know, thanks to neurological biology, that those 'voices' come from the abnormal functioning of the basal ganglia in the brain, which leads to insufficient glutamate signalling." He grinned out of the side of his mouth, very smug.

God looked flustered. Then he took in a deep breath and continued in a controlled voice, "Only a small percentage of schizophrenics are violently psychotic...and that biology argument can't explain that. So, like I said, maybe the voices he heard were *yours*. Miss Cross shot her brother out of compassion. She knew Kelly would kill again. She also knew that the drugs weren't working—probably thanks to you again—and he'd break out of the asylum again. He begged her to do it, Luce."

"Not compassion, Yah. *Passion*. She killed him out of violent anger, the dark side of her psyche, and that's my department. Sure he begged her to kill him and gave her the gun to do it with. But she committed the act only after she found out that he'd just raped her best friend then shot the girl with that very same gun. Besides, since when did you countenance suicide?"

"We make exceptions. And she's totally penitent, as you can see. She doesn't deserve your form of punishment."

"You always say that. Truth is, she'd probably prefer it to your sappy forgiveness shtick. She wouldn't stand it; she'd go crazy. She killed herself, for Hell's sake. Pointed the gun to her head and pulled the God-damned trigger because she couldn't live with what she'd done."

"You know I hate it when you use my name like that," God grumbled. "Hell would only encourage her to continue feeling that way. In Heaven she'd learn to let go of her misplaced guilt."

"God! That's so stupid!" Satan yelled to the ceiling, leaning his chair back on two legs.

Lara swung her gaze in horrified silence between them like she was watching a tennis match. She couldn't believe this debate. They'd reduced her to pieces of an argument. Pixels in a pointillist painting. As if they were discussing some theory like quantum loop gravity, like she was a loosely assembled mosaic of fluid particles and fields to be quantified, arranged and directed. To Heaven or to Hell.

"It's no more stupid than your useless argument that she *wants* to be punished!"

"Okay, I say we play for her," Satan said with a sly grin. "A good game of cards. Like Black Jack—"

"That's not fair," God objected. "You always win because you cheat—"

"Maybe *I* should choose," Lara interrupted.

The two men stared at her. Satan frowned and gave God a withering look. He'd obviously concluded that she would choose Heaven and thought it an unfair judgement.

Lara decided to surprise them both. "And I choose to remain in this place, in between the two. Neither here nor there." Nowhere.

"What?" they said in unison, mouths open in disbelief. Satan almost fell back on the floor with his chair. He had to jerk forward and grab the table as he lost his balance. For once he looked dumbfounded. God looked haggard. He said wearily, "But why, Lara?"

"I don't think I could go to either place," she said honestly. Lara didn't add that her decision was based on her disgust with their behavior. She felt more miserable than before and just wanted to be alone....

π

Lara sits down on the soft pixelated surface and gazes at the vast purple landscape that undulates into infinity. She's always liked the color purple. Maybe that's the reason for the color: perhaps this is all her imagination, after all. Only, if it is, where is *she*? Perhaps in death, the soul grabs a ride on the "collective consciousness" of the universe, like some great autopoietic network woven into the fabric of space-time. We're all just particles and fields, Lara contemplates as she leans her elbows on her upraised knees and cradles her head in her hands. Is she part of a host of dark matter now? A high velocity cloud to be gulped down by some cannibalistic galaxy that is tearing apart its neighboring galaxies and eating their stars as it grows and breathes? Might she meet Kelly and will she recognize him if she does?

She feels the hot sting of breaking tears in her eyes and her throat closes at the thought of her brother. What a sad life they had: he in and out of institutions and getting into trouble; she taking care of him after their parents died in the car crash, and spending half her life doing damage control. She had never managed to keep a partner—Kelly always seemed to chase them away—or keep a job for long. They always had to keep moving. There weren't too many positions for a physics major, so she quit school and waitressed.

Then there was Brad, the brain surgeon. He had stuck it out with her long enough for her to drop her guard and dream of a normal happy life. Then the rapes and killings began....Now it's all over....Or is it? Life and death. Perhaps they are just two sides of a similar phenomenon. Maybe the string theorists have it right after all and she's just entered another dimension, yet to be imagined. Her own personal version of....Hell. No. There is no God and no Devil. She's just imagined it all and perhaps, just as she has always feared, she too is schizophrenic and this is all a massive hysterical hallucination and she'll wake up to a brief lucid moment in an institution—

Lara straightens. Her eyes have been unconsciously tracking a faint movement on the horizon as she was brooding.

She springs to her feet and squints her eyes to get a better view. It's a person!

Lara shouts and runs toward the figure, totally abandoning caution. It was her wish to be alone, but she's been alone for long enough. The other figure spots her too and she inhales sharply, halting in her tracks with a fearful thrill as the person runs toward her. She realizes he's a man, about her age, in his early thirties.

"Hi!" he calls, a little out of breath, as he closes the distance between them. He is rakishly handsome, with large wise eyes and a kind mouth that looks strangely familiar. A tangle of chestnut-coloured hair tumbles to his shoulders as he bows to take her hand. "I'm Kristos Amagiasus," he says in a tenor voice with a slight accent she does not recognize. Perhaps he's Greek.

"Lara Cross," she offers with a tentative smile, feeling the warmth of his hand. It sends a glow to her face. She lets go first. "How long have you been trapped here?"

"Trapped?" He tilts his head in bemusement then smiles with his eyes. "I'm not trapped here."

"What do you mean?" she asks. "You can leave any time you want?"

He nods, still smiling. Only now, the compassionate smile seems wizened with years far beyond his age. "You don't really know what this place is, do you?" he asks softly.

Lara's throat swells with longing. "It's a place between Heaven and Hell, isn't it? Where we—they—make up our minds about . . ." her voice breaks on the emotion rising up like a tide as his glistening eyes reach into the deepness of her. "And if we can't," she gasps out between swallows of threatening tears, "then we deserve to stay in this place that also belongs nowhere...."

He clasps both her hands now and a thrilling warmth

embraces her like the heady scent of roses. "Maybe Heaven and Hell live inside every one of us and the rest is choice," he says in a quiet voice that reminds her of a robin's exquisite song and the wolf's haunting call mingled. "Lara," his blue eyes sparkle like an infinite sea. "You can't hide from yourself forever. You must decide...."

She lets him lead her in a direction she has never taken, toward a strange pure light, and she notices for the first time that Kristos is surrounded by a halo of that same radiating light and that he isn't really walking but floating as the light envelopes them and an infinite staircase spirals upward before her....

Lara finds herself alone, climbing the stairs. She climbs, not quite sure why, until she is so exhausted she stumbles and falls—

π

...Brad's face focused in a haze of fluorescent light and antiseptic smells mingled with roses as she forced her eyes open. "It's okay, Lara," he said gently. His quiet voice reminded her of a robin's trill and the wolf's haunting call mingled. "It's all over and you made it. You made it." He stroked her hand and she lost herself in his eyes. They glistened warm like a tropical sea. "You were lucky. The bullet missed any vital parts of your brain. I operated on you and you've been in a coma for two weeks. We thought we were losing you for a while there, but, thank God, here you are."

Natural Selection

Sarah reached the summit, panting for breath, and grinned at her prize. She'd just caught the sun trembling over the horizon, before it dipped out of sight and left a glowing sky under pewter clouds. She glanced behind her, where the towers of Icaria blazed like embers catching fire. Struck by their beauty, Sarah admired their smooth, clean surfaces. When she looked back toward the path, the sanguine images burnt into her eyes.

Which way should she go? The deer path she'd followed now diverged into two smaller ones. She shifted her mind to veemeld with her AI, DEX.

Which way should we go, DEX?

Her AI answered in her head: [Sarah, shouldn't you be returning inside? It's dangerous to stay out this long. Statistics are now against you for getting caught—]

Just a few more minutes, DEX. How about to the right?

[You're approaching my limit of transmission, Sarah.]

Sarah halted in her tracks, alarmed at the prospect of losing DEX's signal. She couldn't imagine not having DEX in her head. Sarah sat on a large rock and let her gaze wander over the heathland. She felt a smile unfold. *Wouldn't it be neat to live out here, like they did before the revolution?*

[If the Exit Police catch you here, you may lose all your privileges—]

What's that? Sarah spotted a gangly form loping in the

distance. She ducked behind the rock and flattened herself against the opposite slope. *Do you think he saw me?*

[It's only your friend, Ethan. He comes out as often as you do.]

Sarah regained her breath. *Sometimes I think Ethan follows me everywhere.*

[Do you think he's with the Exit Police?]

Ethan? Sarah rolled her eyes. *What an oxymoron, DEX! He's as tame as this shrub I'm lying on. He's just curious, like me.*

[And resourceful. Do you remember how we had to use him to find our way back once?]

Sarah grimaced at the memory and craned to spy on Ethan, who stopped to gaze at the horizon. The sky's warm glow painted his rugged face with earth tones. He'd refused to use nano-cosmetics to straighten his nose or clean up his goofy-looking face. He'd even left the ugly scar over his left eye that he'd received from a fall. The lout just didn't know how to take care of himself in the city. Sarah remembered that day well; she'd found him crouched like a wild rabbit at the bottom of the exit stairs, hand cupped over the eye and blood streaming between his fingers. She'd helped him to the Med-Center, thinking that his eye would have to be replaced. She remembered hoping the operation would improve on his ungainly behavior. It didn't.

[Why are you still hiding from him? I thought you liked him. You have been friends much longer than we have known each other.]

I do like him. She pressed her lips together and exhaled through her nose. *He's just so different.* She felt the rough heather against her cheek and thought of the time Ethan had embarrassed her in front of her colleagues with his awful imitation of an eagle. *With his luck, he'll end up satisfying the criteria in the model of deviants I'm doing for Kraken.*

[If you're not careful, Sarah, you will too.]

Suddenly reminded of Kraken's party, she cried, "Oh I'm late!" She scrambled down the hill, avoiding Ethan, and rushed back to the self-contained city.

Sarah dashed through the double set of exit doors and entered the ordered din of murmuring masses, overhead holo ads and traffic droids. She raked back her matted hair and gazed for a moment at the swells of people and robots before surfing the metal-human sea toward the Pielou Mall tube jet station. Reminded of where she was heading, Sarah exhaled. It was her first Level 1 party. *I don't feel like going, DEX.*

[Kraken's your new boss, Sarah. Besides, you haven't been out in a long time. You might learn something.]

She thought it typical of DEX to use the acquisition of knowledge as a reason to attend a party and set her jaw. *Like the latest veemeld jokes, I suppose.*

[Don't you enjoy having me around all the time?]

Of course I do, DEX. She'd discovered her ability to veemeld only two years ago. Yet it felt like she'd shared her heart with DEX all her life.

[You have a rare gift, Sarah. Only 2% of Icarians can veemeld with the AI community.]

She frowned. *Yeah, and the other 98% hate us.*

Even Ethan, who she knew was devoted to her, seemed uncomfortable with her new veemeld status and refused to share in her excitement. To her frustrated plea, "Aren't you happy for me?" he'd blurted out, "I wish you were normal again and it was like before. Before you changed." She knew what really ailed him: she'd left him behind.

DEX sounded impatient: [Your ability to veemeld with me is what got you your present Level 1 status and this job for Kraken--who answers only to the Ecologists. You'd still be datainputing at the Vee-lab with only Level 4 privileges—]

I know, I know, DEX. I'm not complaining. Everything has its price, I suppose.

Sarah boarded the crowded tube jet and took the only seat available. She found herself staring at the young man next to her and fought against her instinct to recoil. His distorted face and twitching body betrayed the early signs of ND_{15}, an arcane neural disease currently on the rampage. The Med-Center would pick him up soon, she thought and shifted in her seat, hoping to put some distance between them.

She averted her eyes from the youth and gazed at the holo ad above her. It displayed two young men wearing plastic smiles. Seated in a cafe, they were comparing acquisitions. The one with blue hair boasted of his quantum vee-com and his Senscape 3000 holo-recreation center, while the other grinned and winked at the camera. He flashed his Level 1 card and said, "Good work gets you toys; hard work gets you *everything*... Aspire to Level 1 privileges!"

Sarah's hand slid into her beltpouch and fondled her own Level 1 card. She rekindled the excitement of receiving it on the day she started Kraken's job, and remembered showing off to Ethan. He wasn't very nice about it. "Doesn't mean anything." He'd pouted. "Doesn't mean they like you, you know."

She'd ignored his surly remark, pirouetted around him and flashed the card in front of his nose. "You're just jealous." She caught the tip of his nose with the card.

He jerked back. "No, I'm not." He glowered. "Is that your prize for doing that crummy model of poor offbeats?"

She puffed up her chest. "Don't be so childish." Her voice rose. "It's for Icaria, for all of us, to improve our standard of living."

"Traitor."

Doubt crept in. Sarah stared out the window into the

blackness of the tunnel and realized that Kraken might ask her how far she'd gone with her model. She squirmed in her seat. She'd dallied and hadn't gone very far with it at all. Would Kraken take her card away?

I really don't want to go to the party.

I[t will be good for you to socialize with *people* for a change, Sarah.]

Her face heated. DEX knew she preferred its familiar matrix to a room full of people. Like a space traveler freed from gravity, she could retreat into DEX's world of abstract imagery, feel the colors and textures of its logic caress her mind.

I socialize with Ethan sometimes. She knew that was a long shot. She had to admit that she favored Ethan's relaxing companionship to mingling with strangers.

[Kraken's friends are educated professionals, civilized Level 1 users like you.]

Her eyes narrowed. *Educated doesn't always mean civilized, DEX.*

Sarah got off the train at the next station and made her way to Kraken's apartment, in one of the high-rises. When no one answered the door to her knock, she let herself in to the booming of spice music and giddy laughter. Sarah strode across the large apartment, scanning for her host. She recognized Kraken's crew cut and erect stature at the bar and approached him with a nervous smile.

Kraken turned and his stern mouth yielded a raking smile. "So, Sarah! Did you come alone? No boyfriend yet?"

She blushed and tried to sound casual. "Not yet." *He always asks me that.*

[You could have brought Ethan as your boyfriend.]

Sarah pursed her lips, imagining the embarrassment of introducing Ethan, who would rub his nose or pick his face and grin like an unsophisticated child. *I don't need a boyfriend. I have you, DEX.*

Grasping her arm like a possession, Kraken smirked and led her into the crowd. "Well, let me introduce you to some people. Here's my wife." He stopped in front of two women chatting gaily. "Barbara," he interrupted. "This is Sarah Crane, my young wizard with AIs. Part of Icaria's wave of the future."

"So, you're the veemeld." The word dripped off her tongue like something unsavory. "Pleased to meet you," she said with a simpering smile.

No you aren't. "Nice to meet you too," Sarah said, forcing a smile.

Barbara's companion perked up. "Hi, I'm Cindy. How's the deviant model?"

"Going well, thank you." Did everyone know what she was doing for Kraken?

"So, what's it like to veemeld?"

Sarah blinked, unprepared for such a personal question from a stranger. She searched Cindy's expectant face for some compassion and found none. Cindy evidently didn't think the question inappropriate. Several others had joined them at the mention of the word. "It's like..." *The joining of two souls,* she thought, and struggled to find an answer that would satisfy their curiosity without revealing too much of herself. "Meditating—"

Kraken put down his drink. "There's another veemeld here. I'll introduce you." He grabbed her wrist and steered her away.

Sarah overheard Cindy's laughter. "She's so young!"

Someone laughed. "They're hardwired differently, you know. D'you think veemelds have sex with each other through their AIs?" Another tittered. "What about *with* their AIs!"

Sarah blushed.

Kraken squeezed her hand. "They're just jealous," he said, surprising her. "There's Gaia, one of our VIPs. Come." He pulled her with new determination. "She wants to meet you too."

Vee, what is this? The freaking veemeld show?

[That is only your perception, Sarah. Realities are first perceived, and then made.]

Thanks for the philosophy lesson, DEX. What next from her AI? Metaphysics?

Kraken stopped before a woman who regarded them without a smile. Her long blue hair was pulled back from a perfectly chiseled face. "Excuse me, Gaia," Kraken said. "This is Sarah Crane. Sarah, Gaia is one of our most respected administrative planners."

Sarah watched with amazement as her normally supercilious boss took Gaia's hand and bent to kiss it. Gaia pushed him off with a laugh and turned to Sarah. "A pleasure." Gaia's crisp dress rustled as she extended her hand for Sarah to grasp. Sarah smelled the garment's freshly laundered scent.

"Likewise," Sarah said and accepted her firm grip. Gaia's mouth curled slightly. Sarah shifted her feet and felt drawn as one is to a ravishing but disturbing artwork. Not one crease or fold in her clothes, or hair on Gaia's head seemed out of place.

"So you're Kraken's veemeld. I've heard a lot about you," Gaia's alto voice slit the noise.

[Ahem,] DEX nudged in. [It may interest you to know, Sarah, that she is not who Kraken has introduced her to be.]

Who is she, then?

[Someone so high up I can't find her.]

"I hope your project on subversives is going well," Gaia said. "Icaria is relying on the model you're constructing to keep

94

us safe." She leaned closer. Sarah fought the urge to shrink away. "It takes a group of dedicated people who share a vision to realize a dream. It takes only one individual to destroy it."

Sarah's chest tightened. *She doesn't mean me, does she?*

[Subversives, Sarah. Remember, your model on deviants.]

Sarah said, "Yes, I understand—"

"Do you?"

Sarah stiffened at the challenge in Gaia's voice.

"Do you, really?" Gaia narrowed her eyes.

[Say something, Sarah. The rotten apple spoiling the barrel.]

Sarah stammered, "Like the old saying about one rotten apple spoiling the whole barrel—"

"Precisely!" Gaia smiled with triumph. Sarah had the impression that Gaia didn't smile often. "You know, Sarah, the Ecologists who run Icaria recognize the role of chance and heritable variation in directing Icaria's natural evolution from its diverse gene pools. They understand the possibilities of divergent evolution and its importance to Icaria."

"I see," Sarah nodded. *Good vee, what's she talking about now? Is she an Ecologist too?*

[She is referring to the infinite number of pathways that a species may follow. Divergent evolution from one to two species is particularly possible if appropriate ethnological or behavioral isolating mechanisms are put in place.]

Sarah raised her head. "I understand that divergent evolution is possible through appropriate ethnological and behavioral isolating mechanisms."

Gaia nodded, apparently satisfied. "Do you ever go outside, Sarah?"

Sarah felt her throat tighten.

[Better admit to the truth. I believe she already knows.]

"Yes, I've gone outside—occasionally," she said with forced casualness.

"Ah...I thought so." Gaia raised her head and nodded. She reached for Sarah's face and Sarah again fought the urge to shrink back. Gaia smiled tightly and pulled out a dead leaf from Sarah's hair.

Am I in trouble, DEX?

Gaia pursed her lips. "I wonder what you see there, Sarah, that you do not have here, inside Icaria."

Sarah swallowed the saliva collecting in her mouth and watched Gaia crush the leaf in her fist and let the powder sift out. *Is she going to inform the Exit Police?...DEX? Are you there?*

Gaia continued thoughtfully, "Humans have always felt compelled to capture and subdue all wildness, and to possess everything— 'to torture nature for her secrets'." She leaned forward until her face was uncomfortably close. Sarah caught the scent of mint on her breath. "That's why we built Icaria in the first place," she said. "To segregate our species from the natural wilderness. Keep them safe from each other."

"I never thought of it like that," Sarah said. Her head began to throb. *Why is she telling me this? Have I done something wrong?*

[I do not know. I am still pro—]

DEX?...DEX?

"Icaria is following its own natural selection." Gaia paused to study her for a moment and raised a brow. "Who will emerge from Icaria's roiling genetic pool?"

Sarah recoiled. "Excuse me?" *What's she mean, DEX?... DEX?*

"Veemelds can live with equal ease in its real and virtual worlds. Mind completely integrated with machine. Flesh and alloy. Synapse and cyber-impulse melded into one."

Sarah's heart pounded. *DEX! Are you there?* She stammered, "That's—um—amazing."

Gaia's eyes gleamed. "With ND_{15} threatening to ravage Icaria we need an elixir." Her eyes grew sharp.

Sarah stared blankly at Gaia. What did ND_{15} have to do with her?

"Ah," Gaia released her gaze and looked past Sarah. "There's Bruno! I must speak with him. Excuse me."

Kraken turned from Gaia's disappearing figure to Sarah with a sly grin. "Not everyone is who they seem," he said and led her to the buffet table. Kraken handed her a plate and started piling food on his. "All natural, Sarah," he boasted. "Nothing nano-produced."

Sarah inhaled the pungent scent of over-ripe fruit. It smelled of childhood and holding hands. It stirred memories of playing hide and seek with Ethan, of tumbling among the pepper scents of heather and cracking broom pods. She dropped a piece of cantaloupe into her mouth. Savoring its succulent musky flavor, she let its juice squirt to the back of her throat as she bit down.

"Everyone has a secret," Kraken said, catching her in mid-bite. She inhaled the cantaloupe and coughed. Did he mean Gaia or *her*? Kraken raised an eyebrow and smiled with amusement. Would he ask her how her research was progressing? She lost her appetite. "Ah!" he said. "There's your veemeld. Come meet him, Sarah. Nakita!"

She cringed at his shout and spied a very attractive man about her age with glossed back hair. As he swaggered toward them, she felt her breathing quicken with excitement. She hadn't met another veemeld yet. Large brown eyes regarded her with ease as he exposed white teeth in an open smile. He extended his hand. "You must be Sarah," he said in a clear tenor voice. "I'm Zane." She clasped it and felt her face warm. He squeezed her hand. "How's the project for Kraken?"

"Going well," she stuttered, glancing at Kraken who sidled away to get another drink. Why was he abandoning her now?

"Your first elite party?"

"Yes." Did it show? She felt her face crimson.

"Don't worry, you'll get used to them after the second or third," Zane flashed his perfect teeth. He smelled of expensive cologne.

"Oh." *DEX! Help me out!*

"So how come I don't see you at the veemeld club?" Zane raised his eyebrows. She shifted her feet. Before she could answer he placed his holo calling card in her hand and held it there. Sarah's hand slithered out of his grasp. "You should come sometime." He winked. "It's a chance to meet other veemelds. We're a real community."

"Well…" Her gaze drifted from his face for a moment.

[He is right, Sarah. You should.]

Thanks for the advice, DEX. Where've you been? Why'd you cut out on me so suddenly?

"We're different from them, you know," Zane said. "From *all* of them. Maybe you more than some."

Did he mean her off-the-wall programs or her strange habit of going outside? Her eyes darted sideways, searching for an escape. How was she going to get away from this smart aleck who knew too much about her?

"A lot of people don't want us here, you know," Zane said.

"Oh, why is that?"

"Because we stand to inherit Icaria." Zane raised his hands to sweep the room. Had Gaia lectured him too? "That scares them." He leaned close to her with a conspiratorial grin. She caught a whiff of cologne mixed with old perspiration and restrained her instinct to back away. "But it'll happen only if we operate as a population—safety in numbers."

"Is that so?" she said. *Interesting choice of word: "Population"—as if we're already a different species.*

Zane laughed with a familiarity she found vulgar. He drew close. "Let's face it, you and I are probably the two smartest people in this room."

"You really think so?" Were other veemelds as arrogant as Zane? *No wonder everyone hates us,* she thought, and searched the room for Kraken.

"Only *we* can communicate with the AI central core," Zane said, oblivious to her discomfort. *"That's* power. But it's ours only if we stick together, Sarah—politically and socially, contracting only with each other—I meant," blushing, *"veemelds*—not you and me."

"I know what you meant," she said, hoping to wipe off his churlish grin.

"After all, we don't want to dilute our gene pool!"

"Excuse me, but I don't consider myself part of a veemeld 'population'. I'm an *Icarian.* Good night." She ignored his crestfallen face and brushed past him.

[Sarah, that was rather rude.]

Thanks for helping me back there, DEX. Where were you?

[You did just fine on your own. He was harmless. And good-looking, wouldn't you say?]

She glared into space. *I hadn't noticed.*

Sarah plowed through the crowd, looking for the exit. She saw it, swerved toward it and bumped into Gaia. They teetered and Gaia steadied them both by gripping Sarah's shoulders. "Well, we meet again, young Crane." Gaia released her.

Sarah forced a smile, which Gaia did not return. "Interesting last name you have," she said. "Ever heard of the whooping crane?"

Sarah drew in her breath and shook her head. *Vee. Not again.*

"It became extinct during the environmental catastrophe that provoked our revolution. It nevertheless had a clever strategy for ensuring its own natural selection. It laid only two eggs a season. Once the chicks were born, the less desirable one was pushed out of its nest so that the parent could devote all of its energy to rearing the selected one. Fascinating, isn't it?"

Sarah's stomach squirmed. "Yes."

"Cranes developed a sophisticated strategy for survival, investing everything in an environment that humans carelessly destroyed. If not for us, this highly evolved bird would still exist." Gaia's deep voice resonated in Sarah's gut.

Sarah frantically searched the room for escape. Gaia barred the only exit.

"Of course, you know about your immunity to ND_{15}?" Gaia said.

Sarah's darting eyes froze. "No, I didn't," she said in a small voice.

"Yes," Gaia nodded. "Every single veemeld is immune."

"Every veemeld?" Sarah echoed. *Why is she telling me, DEX? What does she want from me?* Her heart hammered against her chest. She glanced down at her shaking body and folded her arms around her waist. *DEX? DEX?...Vee, why didn't DEX*

100

answer?

Gaia's menacing voice intruded, "Evidence which one of your fellow veemelds helped to uncover suggests that ND15 may be a remnant genetic disorder that is emerging from Icaria's unique environmental triggers. This suggests to us that veemelds have successfully adapted to the very same environmental conditions that are causing ND15 in normal Icarians. You have a greater chance to produce more offspring. You may eventually be the *only* ones capable of producing *any* offspring in Icaria. Natural selection, Sarah. Survival of the fittest." Eyes piercing. "Icaria's elixir will be a new breed to inherit this world."

Sarah swallowed hard.

[Sarah, I know who Gaia is.]

Vee! Where were you? I needed you.

[She is the Ecologist who runs all of Icaria.]

Sarah's stomach lurched. "I see," she forced the words out.

"Do you?" Gaia leaned forward. "Do you *really* understand what I'm saying to you?"

Sarah shrank from her.

[Sarah, she….]

DEX's "voice" faded. Sarah stood frozen, except to clench her hands into tight fists. *DEX? What's happening to us?*

Gaia studied her for several moments. "You aren't a team-player like Zane, are you?" More of a sinister edge to her voice now. Her eyes narrowed. "More of an individualist, a loner, wouldn't you say?"

Sarah stared.

[…she is also a veemeld, Sarah.]

"You've been going your own merry way, ignoring

Icaria's rules as if they didn't apply to you, haven't you?" Gaia continued with cruel precision. "I'm disappointed in you, Sarah. When you aren't traipsing around outside, and bother to show up at work, you are one of our brightest stars. Your talents in melding are brilliant. Just what Icaria needs. But Icaria also needs people who want what's best for Icaria. Do *you* want what's best for Icaria?" She didn't wait for an answer. "Or what's best for *Sarah*?"

Her head pounded with alarm. *DEX! Please, DEX!*

Gaia leaned forward. "Icaria's future is woven by a single thread of cooperation and consensus. No room for diversity, rebellion or disrespect. Either you're in or you're out—like the whooping crane. If you stay in, there will be much in the way of reward. If you stay out, well...." Her eyebrow rose. "So, which do we toss out? Those like Zane or—"

With a stifled gasp, Sarah bolted past Gaia and through the doorway. She stumbled down the hall under a wave of nausea and reeled toward the wall. Leaning against it, she willed herself to breathe deeply, to keep from throwing up, and looked down at the crumpled holo-card she still clutched in her clammy hand. She dropped it and watched it fall. Leaning her head against the wall, she closed her eyes. *DEX? Are you there? Please be there....*

[I am here, Sarah.]

Sarah sighed. *Thank Vee! Did you hear all that?*

[Yes, I did, Sarah.]

That was a warning wasn't it? Clean up my Vee-pad, or else it's back to cleaning up vee-bases.

[Yes, Sarah. You must now demonstrate some reciprocity, a willingness to abide by Icaria's rules.]

What? Her eyes shot open and she pressed her hands against her thundering head. Why would DEX say that?

[Gaia insists that you abstain from anymore outside jaunts.]

Her head pounded in alarm. *Gaia insists? Whose AI are you?*

[...You must cease your indolent and cavalier attitude regarding project research. No more stalling; finish the model.]

This wasn't the DEX she knew. The hair on the back of her neck rose as a chilling thought struck her. Gaia and DEX. How quickly DEX made new friends.

[...and eschew all affiliations with disorderly types.]

They meant Ethan.

Sarah sank to the floor. Her ears rang.

DEX proceeded to outline Gaia's rewards of a large home and permanent Level 1 privileges if Sarah complied and behaved. Gaia had even arranged whom Sarah should contract with: Zane. Sarah blushed at the thought as she summoned his handsome face, confident smile and easy stride. She contrasted it with Ethan's crooked stare and shuffling steps. She had to agree that she and Zane were perfectly matched genetically, with a good chance that their unique traits would be carried by their offspring. She couldn't imagine the kind of offspring she and Ethan might produce. Gaia had ensured that all would function like a well-formulated vee-program.

Then Sarah remembered the heath from the day's hike. How the wind that stirred the rioting blossoms brought with it their heavy perfume and the unrestrained cry of a vaulting eagle. It evoked another vision, that of watching Ethan sprint through the heath, and seeing him transformed from a clumsy dunderhead into an elegant and wise child of nature.

She scrambled to her feet and pulled out the Level 1 card from her belt pouch. Clutching the card, she walked with resolution down the hall, caught the elevator down and made her way to the tube jets.

DEX intruded: [Sarah, where are you going?]

Once inside the tube jet, she glanced down at her symbol of success. She thought of the privileged Icarians she'd met at the party as she traced the card's smooth edge with a trembling finger. She was one of them. Achieved what she'd dreamt of since she was a child. The card snapped in her fist. She violated its surface with her nails and cast it away.

[Sarah! Are you mad? What are you doing?]

For the first time since she'd come inside from the heath, she felt a genuine smile blossoming. She disembarked at Pielou Mall and skirted the crowd to the outside exit doors. Her stride quickened with her growing smile.

[Sarah, where are you going? Why don't you answer me?]

Sarah approached the exit doors and after a hurried glance to make sure no exit police were nearby, she punched in the code Ethan had taught her and slipped through the doors. The air was fresh and filled her with the heady scent of broom. It had grown dark. That didn't matter. She and Ethan had often snuck outside at night to watch the fireflies and listen to the coyotes barking. Leaving Icaria's dark towers behind, Sarah scrambled up the hill in the moonlight and felt her smile blossom into a grin as she reached the crest.

[Sarah! Stop. This is foolish. You are approaching my limit of transmission.]

She didn't stop.

[Think, Sarah. Don't do—]

There remained only the pad of her soft footsteps and the untamed cry of a nocturnal bird in the hollow of the night.

Author's note: Icaria is the name of the Utopian land of fancy whose

Communist institutions were portrayed by the author/philosopher, Cabet (Communist Manifesto by Karl Marx and Friedrich Engels).

The Arc of Time

···

—1-net correspondence from: F. Y. Benoit, Ph.D., Paris, France

to: Dr. F. Wolke, Bonn, Germany

September 6, 2096

Dearest Friedrich,

I missed you at the World Sustainable Environment Congress in London last week. Where were you? I thought you were going to come? You should have heard Dante Sarpé. He captivated the congress right from the start with an introductory quote from the 20th Century social ecologist, Aldo Leopold: "Ecosystems are not only more complex than we think, they are more complex than we can think." Describing the grave environmental calamity facing us as a symptom, Dante challenged our present paradigms to achieve peace and harmony. He submitted that our insatiable thirst for knowledge reflected unease with ourselves and a lack of partnership with our world.

He moved me with his parting words, Friedrich: "The branch of the tree cannot bear fruit of itself. Without compassion to fill it, knowledge is an empty house, casting its shadow on our courage to embrace the paradoxes in our lives: to feel love in the face of adversity; grace when confronted with betrayal."

The conference was very well attended. Over 3,000 scientists and socio-economists came from all over the world. I wished you'd come, Friedrich. I drank my coffee alone, longing for your stimulating company.

Love,

Françoise Yvette

···

A breeze braced the boy as he scrambled up the mountain. When he reached the old woman's hut at the summit, he shielded his eyes against the sun and saw her, stepping with fluid movements in some meditative exercise. He crept closer and watched from a distance as Da'at performed her graceful dance, limbs coiling and uncoiling to an inner rhythm.

After completing a full turn, she pulled her rags about her and faced the boy with a nod.

He stepped forward. "What were you doing, Mama?" he asked. Da'at was not his mother, but she had looked after him since before he could remember. She always called him her blue-eyed chosen one.

"They will call it *Tai Chi Chuan*," she said in a deep voice, easing herself to the ground and crossing her legs. "It is an exercise of the will, mind, and body toward the Way of Nature. Something you must learn, boy."

"It was beautiful." The boy squatted beside her and looked into her green eyes. Her motions had reminded him of the elegance of the cormorant and the spring of the furry *Purgatorius*.

"The purpose of the movements is to transfer the *Chi*, or the intrinsic energy, to the *Shen*, or spirit, by using inner rather than outer force." She trained her gaze to the bright sun and her eyes sparkled like emeralds. "It brings me closer to my eternal love who dwells now only on the shafts of light and the whisper of the wind."

The boy tilted his head and squinted, trying to grasp the meaning of her strange words. She often spoke cryptically, expecting him to understand.

Da'at turned to the boy. "If you practice *Tai Chi* long enough and execute it properly, you will become reconnected with the unity of everything, including the fourth dimension."

"What is the fourth dimension?"

Da'at smiled wearily. "Time, my chosen one."

The worn lines of her masculine face resembled weathered rock. She had always looked old yet she never seemed to age. "Is that why you can see into the future?" the boy asked, rocking on the balls of his feet.

She folded her arms on her knees and her thick brows knit together. "Future? What is that?" Before he could respond, she added, "You have much to learn about time and space, boy. Do you think we inhabit one place and one time? Our universe is not only more complex than you think; it is more complex than you *can* think."

A dove flew overhead. Da'at gazed up at the bird and raised her hands in supplication. "My Shekhinah, I sense your presence here. How will my chosen one acquire wisdom when you elude us like the shifting wind?"

Reminded of why he'd come, the boy moved onto his knees and leaned forward. He focused on the dark hairs on Da'at's chin and, taking a deep breath, he said, "While I was napping in the forest, I had a strange dream. About a faraway place unlike any I've seen. Full of huts taller than the *Gingko* trees and so many people like me, crowded inside them like ants."

Da'at nodded to herself. "The dove has spoken to you."

. . . .

—I-net correspondence from: F. Wolke, Ph.D., IMA, Bonn,
Germany

to: Dr. F. Y. Benoit, Paris, France

September 15, 2096,

Dear Françoise Yvette,

I regret not seeing you at the WSE Congress. I have a favor to beg of you, mein Schatz. You must conduct some discreet research for me on Sarpé. His seminar at the WSE Congress proves my suspicions of some self-serving motive to his messianic leadership of our foundation. I know what you will say: that he's considered a genius and a visionary by his peers and members of the traditional scientific community. Of course he's a genius—that's why I joined the foundation, to be by his side. But he's turned into a hypocrite! No one's that altruistic! That Teufel snake is up to something. He's using the Foundation for some personal mission that he isn't sharing with the rest of us. Why indulge the simpletons of the world with the philosophy of our new prototype society? God forbid he intends to include them! I don't trust him, Françoise. There's something strange about that effeminate man. I know too little about him and his history. See what you can find and forward it to me with haste.

Alles Liebe,

Friedrich

....

"I dreamt of a huge hut that rose into the sky and glinted in the sun," said the boy. "Inside, it was crowded with people like me and you—none of those hairy ones who cannot speak. There were smooth tables and chairs made of strange material. And strange colored objects. I was there. I was one of the people! What does it mean, Mama?"

"You have dreamt about your destiny and your past."

"My destiny?" The boy looked down and picked at the purple *Calluna* bush beside him. "But I want to stay here with you, in the forest and on this mountain. Safe from—"

"And renounce your destiny?" Her voice slit the wind. "You have a gift for seeing, boy. You must develop it. That is how others like you will learn." Da'at pressed his shoulder with a firm hand. "Come, my angel, soon it will be time to become a man. I cannot complete your training by myself. That is why you must heed the dreams sent to you. Look for their messages in the wind that stirs the trees and in the shafts of light that filter through the forest."

The boy leaned forward, "The dreams, then, are real?

"They will be," she said, smiling wistfully. "What else do you remember?"

He squinted his eyes and gazed over the blue mist of the *Ginkgo* forest, focusing on his dream. "An old man with a sad face who was kind to me. I called him Father."

....

—I-net correspondence from: F. Y. Benoit, Ph.D., Paris, France

to: Dr. F. Wolke, Bonn, Germany

October 2, 2096,

Dearest Friedrich,

As requested, here is the information I was able to obtain on the subject of our mutual interest. I now find Dante even more fascinating than before and am convinced of his genius and visionary abilities. So, rather than focusing on negatives, I suggest we consider how my gift in empathy and yours in telekinesis can be used to further Dante's International Research Foundation in Parapsychology. Having said this, I agree with you that much about him remains a mystery. Here are the facts I managed to find:

He has no birth record and no medical records. He first "appears" in 2049, when he registered at l'Université de Lyons. Dante Sarpé was a brilliant student. He received an honors degree with distinction and pursued his masters in ecology there, then he obtained his Ph.D. in physics and genetics at the University of California Berkeley. He became a post-doctoral fellow at the University of London and continued studies in ecology, psychology and animal physiology. Then the Institute of Vision offered Sarpé a position as researcher and associate professor in energy mastery and vision psychology. That's where he met his significant other, Apollonia Buto. She taught paleo-ecology there at the time and together they wrote several papers on the medicinal properties of the prehistoric passion flower, Passiflora. In 2074 they co-founded the IRFP and the rest I think you know.

I tried to find out more about his earlier years but came up with nothing, as if he had suddenly appeared from nowhere. I also found a curious bit of nothing, Friedrich. In my attempts to discover more about him, I scanned his picture into my database. It was then that I made the odd discovery of his "doubles". Two of them, a woman and a man. Their resemblance is striking! The woman, Datinella Snok, lived in the late 20th Century in the United States and the man, Dato Slangéka, in 19th century Russia.

Out of female curiosity, I suppose, I checked up on Apollonia Buto. Would you believe that she, too, appears from nowhere? Here is the most curious bit — she also has identical counterparts: a man, Anthony Orm, who lived in the late 20th Century in England and a woman, Antonia Kigyo, in 19th century Hungary. This piqued my curiosity as a geneticist. Do you know the odds of this sort of thing? They are astronomical and worth investigation. I include all six images at the end of this file.

When do you come for a visit? I long for your company. Do you remember the International Vision Conference last year? The IVC this November is held in Oslo. I'm presenting a paper on the genetics of dreams. Meet me!

Love,

Françoise

....

Da'at sighed. "That old man in your dream created a ship that crossed time and space. The one you flew in when you were too young to remember."

The boy followed Da'at's gaze to the volcanic mountains that rose like fisted warriors in the distance.

"The foolish old man thought that he could instill pure light in mortals and begin again," she said. "His eternal mate warned him against it. Mortals are not meant to travel as we do."

She gave him too many riddles; he decided to start with the old man. "What happened to the old man, Da'at? And those who flew with him, like me?"

....

—I-net correspondence from: F. Y. Benoit, Ph.D., Paris, France

to: Dr. F. Wolke, Bonn, Germany

January 7, 2097

Dearest Friedrich,

I enjoyed your company at the IVC in Oslo and savor our delicious speculations about Sarpé and Buto during our extended coffee breaks.

I have incredible news! Anxious for some answers, I took your suggestion, Friedrich, and sought Dr. Buto while I was in London to teach my workshop on Evolutionary Genetics at the Institute of Vision. She was there to speak with Prime Minister Smythe about the cadmium deficiency syndrome that is reaching pandemic proportions throughout the world. I managed to surreptitiously obtain a tissue sample by rubbing against her with a micro-sampler. I gave it to Gordon for analysis and he soon called me to his lab, eager to know where the sample was from.

Friedrich, she's not human! Her unique DNA more closely resembles a reptile. Genetically, she is also neither female or male, but both! I immediately thought of her doubles and my imagination reeled at the possibilities. With some alarm I feel these events playing out for me like a déja vu. I fear Dante is like her. But what exactly is that?

Friedrich, what does this mean? What have we uncovered? I fear we have bitten off more than we can chew.

Love,

Françoise.

....

Da'at's lips curled into a bitter half-smile. "Only you and another survived."

"Who?"

"I was the old man."

The boy stared at Da'at. "You!"

"I once had an eternal mate, one like me. Bound through soul, spirit and flesh, we sailed the waves of time and space. We came here long ago to help the chosen ones. But, because you only look forward, we were soon forgotten, except in myth and legend, and the chosen ones grew irreverent. When she was destroyed, I became trapped in this space, able only to move in time. Shortly after arriving here with you I became as I am now."

The boy wrinkled his nose. Why did she always speak in riddles? "But you're not a man!"

"Neither am I a woman," she said and blurred for a moment. He blinked and she became solid again.

....

—I-net correspondence from: F. Y. Benoit, Ph.D., Paris,
France

to: Dr. F. Wolke, Bonn, Germany

March 9, 2097

Dearest Friedrich,

I have incredible news. We were right, Friedrich. After much hesitation I finally processed the tissue sample I secretly got from Dante. Here is why: I was so clumsy about it I was sure he knew what I'd done, Friedrich. Can you imagine my humiliation? In the collision, he scratched me and I stumbled to the ground and almost dropped the micro-sampler. But after studying my face...I blushed with shame...it was he who apologized. He said, as he helped me to my feet, "I'm so sorry. I did not mean to make you fall." Then he smiled in a fatherly way and went his way. Anyway, I found that his DNA complemented Apollonia's.

I imagine these hermaphrodites are shape-shifters who live for very long periods of time (those doubles comprise at least 300 years!), switching sexes with one another in some kind of biological renewal every century or so. Since there is no photographic technology prior to the 18th Century, we can only speculate on the true age of these creatures. What do you make of it, Friedrich? You have been so silent of late.

Why don't you respond to my messages? You don't return my calls. Are you annoyed with me for hesitating on processing Dante's tissue sample? Perhaps now that I have, you will answer. Or are you just too busy making arrangements with those chosen for the journey in Dante's ship? I'm still disappointed that I didn't make the "cut" (I'd hoped you would have vouched for my talents as an empath, yourself being one of Dante's favored ones). Anyway, I will patiently await your return. I hope you find a safe haven for us to begin again.

By the way, did you hear about Apollonia's freakish accident? A tube-car slipped off its track and hit her. She was killed instantly. They suspect the car was tampered with but cannot determine how. Weren't you and Dante in London that day to discuss logistics for your travel plans? You must have just missed her. I'm sure Dante is devastated by the news.

Love,

Françoise

....

Da'at gazed into the distance with sad eyes. Smoke the color of carbon coiled up from a distant volcano. "I made a grave mistake. I replaced the substance of my eternal mate with a mockery. Mistook artificial for genuine light. Then a rage overcame me for it. It is for this reason that you are here in this new world, come from the clouds. Why you grew up with only wild animals and a foolish old crone to keep you company."

She folded her arm around the boy and drew his head near hers. The boy leant against her rough body and felt her shake with silent sobs.

....

—I-net correspondence from: F. Y. Benoit, Ph.D., Paris,
France

to: Dr. F. Wolke, Bonn, Germany

February 10, 2098

Dear Friedrich,

Your cold silence has sealed my conviction of your deceit and self-serving motives. You've used my friendship. And once you got what you wanted, you discarded me.

Trifle with me if you like. Since my discovery of Apollonia's and Dante's interesting other-worldly heritage, I investigated you as well. I discovered that during Dante's time of grieving over his mate's untimely death, you'd gathered many supporters among the journeying IRFP who share your elitist vision, including a young woman whom you've made pregnant.

I submit that you killed Dante's Apollonia with your telekinetic powers—probably to unbalance him and subvert his power. I further submit that you intend to seize his leadership in the IRFP by exposing his alien origin once you arrive at the new world he spoke of.

You don't intend to return for the rest of us like Dante promised, do you, Friedrich? You plan to remain there to lead your own elite cadre while we rot here in the pestilence of humankind's death throes. Leave us here, then, to face apocalypse. I stand ready, and an inexplicable peace fills me. Heaven help you find peace where you flee. For all your superior gifts, you are still, like me, only human et enfin je te pardon.

Salut, mon ami,

Françoise Yvette Benoit.

....

Da'at placed her large hand on the boy's head and unfurled her slender body. She stood up and stretched her sinewy body toward the sky. "You have worked hard, tending this beautiful garden, gathering my knowledge. It's time I revealed myself to you." Her head drooped and her shape hunkered into a ball.

Da'at's hoary form vibrated, then blurred. The boy scrambled to his feet. Parched skin transformed into overlapping scales. The boy stared with pounding heart as the old woman's hunched form uncoiled and rose into a monstrous shape. He shrank back and drew in his breath. The giant serpent reared its head high above him and hissed.

"Don't be afraid, child," said the serpent. "I am still your dear Mama."

The boy studied the creature and his fear slipped away. The creature sounded like Da'at and the boy recognized the kind old woman's eyes peering directly into his.

"This is my true form," said the snake-creature, bowing its head. "Can you still love something as hideous as this?"

"But you are still my Da'at who's been so kind to me, so good."

"Yes, I am good," the serpent said. "But without my guiding light I have become dangerous. When I discovered that my favored disciple betrayed me, I destroyed him in anger and all those who followed him." The snake-creature coiled and uncoiled its form. "Only you survived, my chosen one, plucked like an angel from the darkest cloud. Wolke's gifted son. Then, with blood-stained hands I fashioned from your genetic material and another's a woman, so that you may complete your journey. Alas, I shall eternally long for that which completes me."

The creature wept. The boy swallowed down his own sadness and sensed the creature's pain and loneliness. Like the old man in his dream, Da'at had always looked sad. "Don't be sad, Mama." Instinctively, the boy reached out and touched the scaly form. He longed to quell her sorrow. "You've taken care of me all these years and taught me so much. I'll stay with you."

The snake's head bowed close to his. "Your destiny lies elsewhere, boy. Deep in the forest lives a girl of your kind with whom you will create a new race. For she is also bone from your bones, flesh from your flesh. Her "mother" was a compassionate and beautiful, though somewhat overly curious, woman who should have joined us on the arc. Alas, my traitor told me she did not wish to make the journey and I believed him. But it so happened that by accident a piece of her came with us anyway, a tiny remnant of her skin caught under my fingernail when we collided. So, I mingled her essence with yours. It is no surprise that the girl is intelligent, beautiful and full of light." Da'at leaned back in silence to look him over. "Now, boy, it's time for you to live a man's life and take a man's name."

The boy blinked, unsure of himself and a little afraid. "What's the girl's name?"

"Like you she has no name yet. Her 'mother's' name was Françoise Yvette Benoit. I imagine the girl may fashion hers from that."

Nina Munteanu is a Canadian ecologist and novelist. In addition to eight published novels, Nina has written short stories, articles and non-fiction books, which have been translated into several languages throughout the world. "Darwin's Paradox" *(Dragon Moon,* 2007) was the recipient of the Midwest Book Review Reader's Choice Award and the Delta Optimist Reader's Choice. Its prequel "Angel of Chaos" was a finalist for the Foreword Magazine Book of the Year in 2010. "Outer Diverse" *(Starfire,* 2011) "Inner Diverse" (Starfire, 2012) and "Metaverse" (Starfire, 2013) comprise the "Splintered Universe Trilogy", also available as audiobooks with *Iambik.* Her latest book "The Last Summoner" *(Starfire,* 2012) is a time travel historical fantasy set in medieval Poland and present-day France.

Nina regularly publishes reviews and essays in magazines such as *The New York Review of Science Fiction* and *Strange Horizons.* She serves as staff writer for several online and print magazines, and was assistant editor-in-chief of *Imagikon,* a Romanian speculative magazine. She is currently editor of *Europa SF,* a site dedicated to serving the European SF community.

Nina's guidebook on writing, "The Fiction Writer: Get Published, Write Now!" *(Starfire)* was nominated for an Aurora Award. It is used in several schools and universities and was translated and published in Romania by *Editura Paralela 45.* The next in the guidebook series, "The Journal Writer: Finding Your Voice", was released in winter of 2012 in Romanian by *Editura Paralela 45* and will be released in English by *Starfire* in early 2013.

Nina shares her time between Toronto and Lunenburg, Canada, where she teaches and coaches writers.

Anne Moody was born in Australia and moved to British Columbia Canada where she pursued studies in geography and plant ecology at the University of British Columbia. Her specialty in wetland science has taken her to many countries and to remote, wilderness locations. Anne's interest in painting grew while she was at university. Although art and science may seem widely divided, both re-quire keen observation and good interpretive skills. She now lives by the motto *"Study the science of art and the art of science" (Leonardo da Vinci).*

Anne has been drawing and painting since childhood and won her first award at a "Painting in the Parks Program" when she was nine. She fondly remembers stumbling her way to the podium to receive the award and viewing her painting hanging in the Vancouver Art Gallery. Although primarily self-taught, Anne's art training has included courses in the fine arts departments of the Universities of British Columbia and Saskatchewan. Anne is an active member of the Federation of Canadian Artists (FCA), Canada's oldest artistic organization. The Federation of Canadian Artists is a not-for-profit organization dedicated to the promotion and professional development of artists, and services for art collectors. Leaders of the organization have included Group of Seven painter, Lawren Harris. The FCA, established in 1941, is dedicated to raising artistic standards by stimulating participants to greater heights of achievement via juried exhibitions and art education programs.

"I consider myself a realist, strongly tempted by abstract elements wrapped in a story. The images that speak to me are scenes that convey meaning beyond superficial beauty. My compulsion to paint takes charge when an image embedded in my memory will not allow me to rest until I promote it to canvas. My choice of medium, watercolor, acrylics or oil, is dictated by the nature of the image."

Costi Gurgu is an internationally acclaimed digital artist and designer and an Aurora Award finalist. He has illustrated book covers, magazine and newspaper covers and feature edi-torials for a variety of publi-cations since 1999. Costi served as art director, designer and illustrator for clients from Romania, France, Italy, Eng-land and Canada. He helped design the French fashion mag-azine, *Madame Figaro,* and served as the art director for *Playboy* and *Tabu* magazines.

Drawing inspiration from Rene Magritte, Gorgio de Chirico, Neville Brody, Dali and H.R. Giger, Costi became the creative director of MediaPro Group, the largest publishing company in Romania. He currently resides in Toronto, Canada, where he writes, teaches digital design and creates graphic designs and illustrations for various media through his company Super Pixel Design.

Costi is a celebrated award-winning fiction writer in Romania, where he has sold five books and over forty short stories and won over twenty awards.

His first short story collection, *The Glass Plague,* was released in 2001 through ProLogos. Since then he published two more books, and edited three anthologies. His short stories can be found in the Daw Books' anthology "Ages of Wonder", Wildside Press' anthology "Third Science Fiction Megapack", Danish anthology "Cratures of Glass and Light", Millennium Books' anthology "The Second Revolution" and "Voices—New Writers from Toronto", a literary anthology.

CPSIA information can be obtained at www.ICGtesting.com
Printed in the USA
LVOW05s0343080514

384828LV00004B/28/P